OUT OF HIS LEAGUE

BRIARWOOD HIGH SERIES

MAGGIE DALLEN

Copyright © 2018 by Maggie Dallen

All rights reserved.

No part of this book may be reproduced in any form or by any electronic or mechanical means, including information storage and retrieval systems, without written permission from the author, except for the use of brief quotations in a book review.

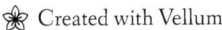 Created with Vellum

ONE

Veronica

FAKE IT TILL *you make it.*

As far as personal mantras go, mine wasn't terribly original, but it was effective. Sort of. At least, I hoped it would be.

Time would tell.

My best friend, Trent, was driving me to my first day at a new school for my junior year. After a lifetime of going to the same school with the same class, I'd been granted an amazing opportunity to start fresh and I was determined to make the most of it.

Physically, at least, I was ready. You know those scenes in cheesy teen romantic comedies where the girl gets a makeover and is totally transformed in a one-minute montage?

Yeah, I'd done that.

Well, my friend Margo had done that. She'd been the one to teach me how to blow out my frizzy, curly brown hair into pretty waves. She'd taught me how to wear makeup and how to walk in heels. But trust me, it hadn't happened in a matter of minutes. It had taken all summer.

Mentally I was prepped, too. I'd been planning for this moment ever since I got my acceptance letter from Briarwood, a private school I scored a scholarship to. It was on the other side of town from my old public school, Atwater, and it might as well have been in a different universe.

No one knew me at Briarwood, which was terrifying, but also incredibly exciting. It meant I had a chance to reinvent myself, and I didn't have to wait until college to do it. Physically and mentally, I was ready to play the part of Veronica Smith—the confident, cool, dateable new junior.

But if I could actually pull it off remained to be seen.

Sitting in the front seat of Trent's car as we neared my new school, it was kind of hard to fake it. Trent knew me way too well. He, like everyone else I'd grown up with, knew me as Ronnie—tomboy, jock, and completely invisible to the male population.

Before you get any ideas, I should say right now—this is not a story about how I fell in love with my best friend. No way. Trent is awesome and I love him dearly—as a brother. So no, and also...ew. I can't even go there in my imagination. I should also probably mention that my friend Margo in the backseat was his girlfriend. They'd been dating since freshman year and since I was Trent's best friend, Margo had become my first and only female friend by default.

I'd been friendly with a lot of the girls on my old soccer team, but soccer was the only thing we'd really had in common, and those friendships had stayed on the field. Besides, any one of my former teammates would have looked at me like I was crazy if I'd asked them to help me with my hair. But Margo? She stepped into the role of my lone girl friend like a champ.

But she wouldn't be my only female friend for long, hopefully. Veronica Smith was going to make friends. Girl friends. And she was going to be noticed by guys. She was going to flirt, and date, and as God as my witness, she was going to have her first kiss.

My inner diatribe was cut short as Briarwood came into view. The butterflies in my stomach went crazy and I sucked in a quick, loud inhale as I clutched my belly.

Trent glanced over. "You all right, Ronnie?"

"It's not Ronnie anymore," Margo scolded from the backseat.

I felt her hands on my shoulders as she leaned forward so her face was next to mine. I already knew I was in for another pep talk. She'd very sweetly come over to my house super early this morning to help me with my hair and makeup.

Despite her many lessons these last few weeks, I still hadn't been confident enough to do it on my own. This morning she'd alternated between making me look good and boosting my confidence.

I was so freakin' glad Trent was dating Margo.

Trent tried to be helpful in his own way, like by offering to give me a ride on my first day so I didn't have to show up on the bus. Still, he couldn't quite seem to get on board with my plan. He didn't understand why I might want something different, to *be* somebody different.

Margo, on the other hand... well, I got the feeling that this was her dream come true. She was a big fan of all those cheesy rom com movies where the nerdy girl becomes popular just because she gets a sweet blowout and a pair of contact lenses.

For Margo, my plan was the closest thing she'd ever experienced to that in real life. And in real life, she got to be the awesome fairy godmother character who gives the makeover.

She was pretty pleased with herself on that front.

I glanced in the side mirror at the still unfamiliar reflection. I was pretty darn pleased, too. She'd done an awesome job. I wouldn't have recognized me if I saw myself walking down the halls of my old school, where Trent and Margo were headed after they dropped me off.

I'd been dying for a change for a while now but trying to change your image when you're surrounded by people who've known you since kindergarten? It's next to impossible. Even Trent couldn't wrap his head around this new me and he knew me better than anyone.

It was Margo who reminded him. "She's going by Veronica now," Margo said, her voice all stern, but still cute. She couldn't help it. Margo was just cute by nature. Small and blonde, she'd always been popular at Atwater. Not in a *Mean Girls* way but in the "I'm nice to everyone" way. In return, everyone loved Margo. Including me. She'd taken me under her wing these past few weeks, helping me to develop my new identity.

"She's Ronnie," Trent said, "And she always will be."

I sighed. That was why this new and improved me could only exist at a new high school. I had to kill off Ronnie. It's not like I was the lowest rung on the social hierarchy. I had some friends—all nerdy boys, except for Margo and my teammates. Trent might have been the nerdiest of them all. It was still a wonder to me that Margo had fallen for him, but I guess he did have a cute grungy rocker look about him that was an oddly good complement to Margo's goody-two-shoes vibe.

My vibe was total tomboy. I'd always been into sports and had been more comfortable hanging out with the boys in my class. I'd never liked shopping, or tight clothes, or taking time to do my hair. I liked being comfortable, and that usually meant oversized T-shirts and frizzy curls scraped back into a ponytail.

And while that was all fine and good for a long time, once I hit high school I didn't know how to break out of that image. And here's the thing... I wanted to go on a date. I wanted to be kissed. And yes, one day I wanted a boyfriend. I didn't want to go through my entire life being treated like a boy just because I'm good at sports and don't know the first thing about highlights and lowlights.

So when I got the scholarship offer to go to Briarwood, I seized on the chance to start fresh. Just thinking about the clean slate ahead of me made the butterflies ease up, excitement taking their place.

It was hard to not feel like a fraud, but as Margo liked to point out—I wasn't being a fraud, I was just being a better version of me. Because while I liked sports, there was more to me than just that. I was also a good baker and had great grades. I liked to read romance novels and I adored old movies. I wrote for the newspaper back in my old school and dabbled in photography.

I was more than just a tomboy, just like Trent wasn't just a computer nerd with a thing for indie bands. But I guess when you're stuck in the same building with the same group of people, you get put in a hole. You get stuck with your label and it's almost impossible to break free.

There were a lot of reason I wanted to go to Briarwood —great soccer team, better chance at getting into a college of my choice, better teachers—but starting fresh was the biggest one.

Trent pulled up in front of the school, which looked daunting with its ivy-covered walls. Margo kneaded my shoulders like a coach, which she kind of was. She was my cool-girl coach. "You've got this, Veronica."

It was a bad sign that my full name sounded weird to me, wasn't it?

No. I'd get used to it.

Trent sighed. "I still don't get why you want to be different. You're the coolest girl I know, and—"

Margo and I both slapped his bicep and he winced. "Aside from Margo, obviously."

Margo grinned and planted a kiss on his cheek. But he was focused on me, his eyes sweetly squinted with concern beneath his black-framed glasses. "Ronnie, you don't need to change who you are just to be liked by some guy."

I held back a sigh as Margo groaned and flopped back in her seat. We'd all been over this so many times, it was getting super old.

"I'm not changing who I am just to get a guy," I said for the millionth time.

"She's being herself, just in a way you're not used to," Margo chimed in.

I pointed back to her—Margo got it. "Exactly. I'm being me, just... a new me. I want to be all of me."

Trent looked unconvinced.

"I'm fun, right?" I asked.

He nodded. "Yeah, of course."

"And I can flirt...I think." I'd never really tried because there were no guys in my old high school who wanted to flirt with me.

"I'm sure you can," my ever-supportive Margo said.

Trent rolled his eyes. I think it icked him out to think of

me flirting just like I didn't particularly like to think about what he and Margo got up to during their sexytime.

I'm serious when I say that Trent was the brother I'd never had. And I guess Margo was kind of like the sister I'd never had. So together? Ew. I couldn't go there.

I shook off the horrid thought and focused on the conversation at hand. "And I am a girl, right? So why shouldn't I have fun and flirt with boys?" I grasped Trent's hand, outright pleading with him to understand. "Just once I want a guy to look at me like I'm a girl. I want to be invited to parties that aren't a bunch of dudes playing video games."

"You like video games," he pointed out.

I rolled my eyes. "Of course I like video games, but every once in a while I'd like to go to a party where there are girls there and dancing and spiked punch and—"

"And you have watched too many movies," Margo said with a laugh. "No one has spiked punch at house parties."

I waved her off. "Fine. Beer. Whatever. I just want to experience what it's like to be popular and..." *Wanted. Noticed. Seen.* "And liked for something other than my skills on the field or as a gamer."

Trent looked like he might relent, but he still had concern in his eyes. "But you're not going to stop playing soccer, right?"

I shook my head. "Of course not. I love soccer, and volleyball, and softball—I'm not giving them up. I just don't want that to be all that defines me."

At this point, my monologue was on automatic. We'd gone through this before. So. Many. Times. I loved the fact that he loved me just as I was, but in a way Trent's view of me was part of the problem. He'd never see me as anything other than his old pal Ronnie, and I couldn't wait to be surrounded by people who didn't know me at all.

I glanced up at the school and watched as a stream of students filed out of cars and into the big double doors. An entire school full of people who didn't know me.

This was my dream come true.

"Fine," Trent relented, reaching into the backseat to grab my book bag. "Let me know how it goes today."

"I will."

"And tell Drew I say hello."

His words stopped me as I was reaching for the door handle, a sick feeling started to well up in my gut. "Drew?" I turned around to face him. "Who's Drew?"

I could only think of one Drew. As far as I knew, Trent and I both only knew one Drew.

Relax, Ronnie. Maybe this Drew was a musician who Trent knew from seeing local bands or something. Maybe he was a friend of the family or—

"Drew Remi," he said.

The name made my stomach heave. Drew Remi. As in the same Drew who'd gone to school with us up until first semester last year, when he'd moved away.

"Drew moved to California," I said. From what I'd heard, his mom had gotten a job in Los Angeles and Drew had moved there with her. My friends and I had been jealous when we'd heard that he was leaving cold Pennsylvania behind for sunny California. Most of the girls in our class had gone into mourning, but no one had whined and wailed more than his girlfriend, April. Or ex-girlfriend, I guess. After he'd left, she'd stopped moaning and started dating another one of the popular guys in our class.

But no one had been more popular than Drew Remi. He'd been an A-lister, if such a thing exists outside of Hollywood. He'd been athletic, hot, and charming...or so I heard. I hadn't had much to do with him since junior high. Before that point, we'd all been friends. But once puberty hit, it was a whole other story. Everyone separated. Drew had become super popular and I... had not.

"He and his sister didn't stay in California long. They moved back to town last spring and started at Briarwood," Trent was saying this as though it was no big deal. Like he was just mentioning that it looked overcast outside. *Hey, it might rain today. Also, your whole plan at reinventing yourself is doomed to fail. Have a great day!*

"I didn't know that." Margo was looking at Trent with the same look of horrified outrage I wore, though why Margo was upset was not nearly as obvious to me.

For me, this could ruin everything.

She swatted his shoulder. "You should have told me."

Ah. It was a couple thing, apparently. I shook my head. I couldn't worry about their squabbles at a time like this.

"It's not a secret," he said. "But it doesn't have anything to do with us or our friends. Sounds like he has a new crew these days. New school, new team, new girls." Trent shrugged as if this was obvious.

"Why didn't he come back to Atwater?" Margo asked.

He shrugged again. "I don't know. Probably because Briarwood has the better baseball team."

Ugh. I'd forgotten that he'd been an up-and-coming baseball star when he'd left our school.

"So he doesn't see his old friends anymore?" Margo asked. "What happened?" She was clearly in info gathering mode whereas I was just trying to quell the burgeoning panic attack. I was here. I was all decked out in new clothes, with new makeup and a freakin' blowout that took forever to perfect.

This could not be all in vain just because Drew freakin' Remi decided he didn't like California.

"Maybe he hangs with some of his old friends," Trent hedged. He clearly had no idea. Drew's 'old friends' meant that elite little clique that ruled my former public school with their trendy clothes and effortless confidence. Trent didn't hang out with that crowd, and while Margo was friendly with some of the A-list girls, she didn't party enough to be in their inner circle and apparently that satellite status meant that she'd missed a key bit of gossip.

A totally relevant bit of gossip that could change everything.

"You guys, focus," I said.

Both heads swiveled so they were facing me. Trent still looked confused, but Margo had that look of determination I loved so much.

It meant she had a plan.

"He won't recognize you," she said.

Trent and I stared at her. I finally broke the silence. "Margo, I went to school with Drew from kindergarten through freshman year. I think he knows who I am."

"She peed her pants at his birthday party," Trent helpfully added.

Margo turned to me and I threw my hands up. "I was five! And this is not the time to rehash old embarrassing stories, Trent." I gave his shoulder a shove that made him grunt.

"Sorry," he mumbled. Turning to Margo, he added, "But the point is. He's going to know who she is." Then to me, "I just don't see what the big deal is. So Drew knows. That's a good thing, right? You'll have a ready-made friend."

Margo and I shared a look of exasperation. She was the only one who understood what I was trying to achieve here. A new me. A clean slate. Bye, bye Ronnie the tomboy. Hello, Veronica the dateable. Veronica who did normal girl things with normal girls. Veronica who got attention from boys for something other than her ability to dribble and hold her own in *Fallout 4*.

"She doesn't want a ready-made friend," Margo said.

"Also," I piped up. "He and I were never friends. At least, not since fifth grade. Why would he suddenly want to be my friend?"

"Because you're hot." Trent's face split in a grin I'd never seen before. The way he was looking at me was gross. "Seriously, what did Margo do to you? You look like a... like a..."

"Like a girl?" I finished.

He nodded. "Yeah." Then his gaze met mine and he scowled. "It's weird."

I shrugged. "Get used to it."

Margo leaned forward so her head was jutting between us, effectively cutting off this new bickering match before we could rehash the same argument for the millionth time. "Trent just made my point for me."

He frowned at me. "I did?"

I frowned at him. "He did?"

Margo nodded confidently. "He did. My doofus of a boyfriend here is right." She grasped me by the shoulders so I was forced to turn awkwardly to face her in the back seat. "You. Are. Hot. Trust me when I say that he won't recognize you."

She looked so sure of herself and her makeover abilities, I didn't have the heart to argue. But I caught Trent's look over her shoulder. He wasn't convinced, and neither was I. Drew and I might not have been friends but we'd known each other forever. Makeup and hair wouldn't erase that.

I forced a smile for Margo's sake. "Maybe you're right." And even if she wasn't, it was fine. I would just steer clear of him. He'd managed to ignore me for years before he left our school; surely he'd do the same now.

And I'd do the same. Ignore, ignore, ignore.

I flipped down the overhead mirror on the car's sun visor and gave my new and improved face one last look.

I looked good. I looked like a girl. I looked... nothing like me.

But this was the new me, I reminded myself just like I'd reminded Trent.

Get used to it.

TWO

Drew

ONE OF THE guys from the football team slid in next to me at the cafeteria table. "Dude, have you seen the new girl?"

He was making a scene, leaning back so far he looked like he might fall over as he tried to seek out the hot new girl who everyone had been talking about since first period.

Briarwood was a small school, way smaller than the public school I went to for about half a second in California, and even a little smaller than Atwater, my old public school on the other side of town.

I hadn't seen the new girl yet, but I'd heard all about her. Hot, seemed to be the consensus among the guys. Friendly and sweet was what I'd heard from Melody, the school's biggest gossip and self-proclaimed one-woman welcome wagon. She'd been the one to greet me my first day, most likely to get the scoop on me firsthand, and I had no doubt she'd done the same to this new girl.

I had to admit I was curious.

Brian hit my arm and it stung. I was no wuss, but sometimes Brian forgot his own strength. The guy was a brick wall, which was a great asset on the football field. In the cafeteria? Not so much.

"She's over there at Melody's table. Check her out. She's totally your type."

I resisted the urge to look over. I didn't have a type. Not anymore. And especially not now when the playoffs were coming up. I couldn't afford to lose focus when we were two games away from being state champions.

I held out as long as I could, but then Alex and Ted sat across from me. My buddies from the school's summer league baseball team were talking about... you guessed it. The new girl.

"Man, I'm going to talk to her by the end of the day," Alex said. "I need to get in there before anyone else does. She's totally my type."

"I thought your girlfriend was your type," I said, digging into the fries on my plate. I'd had an early morning pitching practice that made me miss breakfast. I was starving. Besides, focusing on the fries helped me resist the urge to follow everyone else's stares. I'd see the new girl soon enough but right now I didn't want any distractions, and I also didn't want to be one of the many who were leering at the poor girl. I'd been the new kid twice in the past year and trust me, it sucked. First days were the worst. The stares, the whispers. I wouldn't be hypocritical and say I wasn't curious about the girl everyone was talking about, but I sure as hell didn't want to add to her first day miseries.

Alex reached over and stole one of my fries. "Naw, Tina and I broke up."

Again. That part went unsaid. It was a struggle not to

roll my eyes. No one had more girl problems in his life than Alex—he and Tina seemed to break up every other day. I couldn't imagine why he was seeking out more drama, but then, what did I know?

I hooked up with girls now and again but I'd learned my lesson on high school relationships—they were doomed to fail. And high school girls? Forget it. They were hardwired to play games and mess with your head.

I had no desire to have my head messed with again, and if I wanted games, I'd play them on my Xbox.

There were plenty of girls who were happy to just hookup at parties, maybe hang out and have some fun. That was all I was looking for, and right now, even that sounded like too much work. I had to stay focused on my game, so girls—*all* girls—were off limits until summer league playoffs ended.

I made it all through lunch without sneaking a peek, even though the conversation never strayed far from this Veronica chick. It was a freakin' gossip session as the guys spilled what they'd learned from their various sources.

It wasn't much. No one seemed to know where she'd transferred from or what she was doing at Briarwood. So far the most salacious tidbit was that she'd gotten into some AP classes. Whoa, stop the presses! I kept my mouth shut, but seriously? How boring were their lives if these guys were gossiping like a bunch of old grandmas about some new girl's course load?

I was relieved to head out of there when the bell rang. By last period that day, I'd successfully avoided seeing the new girl, though her name was still being bandied about by just about everyone in the school.

I felt sorry for her, to be honest. If there was some way I could help her to feel welcome, I'd have done it, but I didn't want to be yet another guy trying to get her attention. From the sounds of it, she'd been hit on by every guy in school by now.

By all accounts, she was sweet about it. Nice and polite, all smiles and pleasant chit-chat with everyone, even the biggest dorks and the largest outcasts. From all the talk, she was starting to sound too good to be true.

Then I found out for myself that the rumors were false. Sweet and friendly? Hardly.

Or, maybe it was just me.

I ran into her. Literally. Books fell, and I nearly bit my tongue off as my jaw clamped shut at the collision. The next thing I knew, a soft, warm body was in my arms as I caught my balance... and her.

I stared down into big brown eyes. Long dark lashes batted up at me. Her lips were a soft pink and they were parted in surprise.

I wasn't sure how long we stood like that, oddly posing as though we'd planned this. She'd come running down the hall, fall into my arms, and I'd dip her like we were on stage for a ballroom dance competition.

Obviously, that wasn't the case, but there I was, holding her in a dipping pose as she clung to my shoulders. There was something familiar about her, like I'd known her my whole life. There was a kindness in her eyes, a softness to her features that made me smile instinctively, wanting to see her smile in return.

And she smelled good, like some sort of citrus shampoo or body wash or something. Damn, I wished I hadn't noticed that. I was already too dumbstruck by the looks of her. I didn't need to have an intoxicating scent paired with her too.

And I definitely wished I didn't know how good she felt in my arms.

The bell rang for the start of class and the moment was over. I was righting her. She was scrambling for her books on the ground. The whole incident couldn't have lasted more than a few seconds but for me, it felt like time had stood still.

I took a deep, steadying breath before going down on my knees to help her pick up her books. We were both heading in to AP Literature and I knew Ms. Davies would be pissed if we were late.

"Here, let me help you," I said.

She muttered something that I didn't hear. Her long brown, wavy hair fell forward and I couldn't see her face. Even though I couldn't see her face, I could see the way she hunched in on herself, as if she was trying to hide from me. Oh hell, almost like she was scared of me.

"Hey," I said as gently as I could, placing a hand on her arm. "I'm sorry about that. Let me help you."

She shook me off with surprising strength and this time I heard her voice, low and short. "I said I've got it."

I sat back in stunned silence and watched her gather the last book before turning quickly, avoiding making eye contact. Then she headed into the classroom without me.

"Mr. Remi." Ms. Davies' voice was an unamused monotone. "Being late on your first day is inadvisable."

I got to my feet, grabbed my stuff, and went in. So that was the new girl everyone was talking about. The one who was beautiful, friendly, and kind to everyone she met.

Beautiful? Check. But friendly and kind?

Maybe she was nice to everyone who wasn't me. In fact, I was pretty sure I was the exception to the rule. How did I know? I watched her. All through class I stared at her, listening as she smiled and chatted with everyone who talked to her when there was a break in class and at the end when the bell rang. She was the center of attention and there was never a moment when someone wasn't trying to get her attention.

She was never anything but friendly and kind, but the whole time she pointedly ignored me even though we were assigned seats right next to one another.

What the hell? Who was this chick and what had I ever done to her?

THREE

Veronica

HE DIDN'T RECOGNIZE ME.

I laid on Trent's unmade bed as he and Margo pestered me with questions about my first day. I stared up at the glow-in-the-dark stars on his ceilings that I'd helped him put up so many years ago. I was having a hard time focusing on the rest of the day because my mind kept going back to that one incident.

The incident.

He hadn't recognized me. I still couldn't believe it.

First of all, how utterly ridiculous that when I did finally run into Drew, I literally ran into him. I was not a clumsy person. At all. I mean, just look at all my trophies. I'm no ballerina, but I'm not a klutz either. So the fact that I ran into anyone at all was weird. But why did it have to be *him*?

My mind kept replaying that moment when I was awkwardly hanging out in his arms. Literally, hanging. The look on his face... I could have sworn he recognized me. He looked stunned, obviously, but there was a recognition there. And then he'd smiled.

Oh man, that smile.

I'd forgotten how cute he was. No, not cute. He'd been cute as a freshman, but now? Now he'd grown up. He'd filled out and the boyish features had solidified into something manly. His jaw was sharper, his cheekbones more defined.

And his body? Yeah, that had definitely filled out. He was still tall and lean, but I felt the hard chest and the muscles that had bulged beneath my touch as he'd lifted me back up to my feet as if I weighed nothing.

I let out a long breath.

"Are you all right?" Trent asked.

I glanced over to see them hovering around me with matching looks of concern.

"You're kind of catatonic," Margo informed me. "Do you need some water or something?"

I shoved myself up onto my elbows. "No. No water. I just... I need to regroup."

Yes. Regroup. That was what I needed. Margo sat beside me, her hands fussing with my hair. I hated to tell her that I no longer needed to look pretty and that in about two point five seconds all that perfectly blown out hair would be tossed up in a bun. And these clothes? They were so gone as soon as I got home.

God, how did those A-listers in my old school do it every day? The hair, the makeup, the tight clothes? It was exhausting.

I met my gaze in the mirror. *Get used to it.*

I bit back a groan. Today was only day one of a long school year. *Two* long school years, but at least there'd be a summer in the middle there. A summer during which I intended to let all of the hair on my body do whatever it wanted.

That included my leg hair. Unless I was going to the pool or the beach. I may not be a beauty queen but I didn't want to scare any small children either.

Before the questions could start up again, I gave them a recap of my day. It had been a success, hands down. Until I'd run right into Drew Remi... and he hadn't recognized me.

"See?" Margo squeaked, looking entirely too pleased with herself as she shot a triumphant look at Trent and then me. "I told you he wouldn't recognize you."

Trent shook his head. "I don't believe it."

Me neither! "Believe it," I said.

"Are you sure he just couldn't place you?" Trent said. "Maybe he couldn't remember your name."

I thought about that. At first I'd thought he'd recognized me, but then... that smile. Holy hell, I'd know that smile if I'd seen it before, and I had never seen anything like that from Drew Remi. It wasn't friendly so much as it was sexy. And it wasn't a smile that said, "oh hey, I know you from somewhere." It was a cocky grin with a sultry drawl that said, "hey girl, I'd like to get to know you."

And yes, I totally gave his smiles voices. I'm not sure when that happened, but my imagination had gone a bit wild after that run-in and his smile, the look in his eyes, the way he'd felt, the way he'd smelled—it was apparently all I could think about.

I should have been thinking about my game plan. I should have been celebrating my success. All those self-help books had been right. It had been so easy. All I'd had to do was fake it... and I'd made it.

For one day, at least.

I'd held my head high and pretended that I was totally comfortable with my surroundings. And guess what? Everyone bought it. Walking into the cafeteria was terrifying but I made sure to keep a calm smile in place despite my sweaty palms and two seconds into my terrifying walk down popularity plank I'd been hailed over to sit with a group of girls who were clearly at the top of the pack.

Ugh, listen to me. Walking the plank? Top of the pack? First of all, I was massively mixing metaphors, and second of all, I was falling into the trap of thinking that high school is just one big popularity contest. Which, it kind of was, but it didn't have to be. Right?

"This is a good thing, right?" Margo asked, drawing my attention back to planet earth and her big, blue excited eyes. "I mean, you didn't want Drew to recognize you, and he didn't. Mission accomplished!"

She was watching me with excited anticipation. Trent? Not so much. He looked wary and like he wanted to argue with his girlfriend, but wouldn't.

Wise man. Margo seemed awfully invested in this one.

And I knew why. She'd invested in me. She'd spent a good deal of time and energy helping me to be *the best version of me.* "The best version of me." Ugh. I was getting tired of hearing that phrase. She'd stolen that line from one of my self-help books and she'd run with it. Now it was one of her favorite sayings. I supposed it was better than the alternative: "I helped Ronnie go from ugly to passable."

Equally true and not nearly as nice.

I forced a smile for her sake. "Right."

No. Wrong. I mean, yes I'd hoped to stay off his radar, but to come face to face with him and have him not recognize me?

It hurt. My pride stung. I knew I hadn't been popular at our old school, but I hadn't thought I'd been so very forgettable. I mean, was I really *that* invisible? Had anyone outside of Trent and Margo even noticed I wasn't there today?

I almost asked but lost the nerve.

Neither Trent nor Margo was a good liar. If no one had noticed I was gone, they wouldn't be able to hide the truth. They'd hesitate at the very least before trying to lie. And honestly, I wasn't sure my ego could take that. So I didn't ask.

Instead I made myself feel better by remembering that Atwater's girls' soccer team would start up this week and my team would notice I wasn't there. I'd been one of the stars of the team. At least there was one area where I knew I'd be missed.

Briarwood's soccer season started this week too and I couldn't wait. I hadn't mentioned it to the girls I'd had lunch with today because I was determined that I was going to be known for more than just that at my new school. I could be well rounded, dammit. I *was* well-rounded. I just couldn't get anyone to see that before now.

Trent didn't look fooled by my answer. "Ronnie, don't worry about Drew. He's not worth your time, anyways. I asked around about him today. Sounds like he's ignoring all his old friends." He made a face of disgust. "Just because he's going to Briarwood now and is their starring pitcher he thinks he's too good for us or something." His eyes meet mine. "No offense."

"None taken." The Briarwood kids had something of a reputation in my old school for being stuck up and elitist. But then the two schools were kind of rivals so I'd decided to take that with a grain of salt. From what I could tell at school today, the students at Briarwood were pretty similar to those at Atwater, for better or for worse.

But people see what they want to see, I guess.

For me, Briarwood was more of the same. Just like Atwater, it was a high school filled with teenagers who cared about what other people thought—me included. I wasn't all high and mighty about it. I gave up trying to pretend that I was above it all.

I wanted to fit in. I wanted to be popular for once in my life. I wanted to be noticed.

The way I saw it, Briarwood was a practice round for college. Everyone knew that college was a chance to reimagine your identify. But I didn't want to wait. And now, thanks to my scholarship, I didn't have to.

"This is a good thing," Margo insisted. "If Drew didn't recognize you than he can't cramp your style. All you have to do is steer clear of him." She clapped her hands together as if that was all settled. And maybe it was. She had a point; I was being ridiculous. I didn't want him to recognize me but then when he didn't I moped about it?

Totally nonsensical.

Margo was already moving on to more interesting topics. "Other than Drew Remi, how'd it go?"

I grinned. "Great. It went perfectly." And it had. Drew Remi aside, I'd had more guys talk to me in one day than in my entire life.

She listened with excitement as I detailed my day, from being greeted by a queen bee in the first minutes of arrival to being hit on by a hottie named Alex. Twice, actually. The All-American boy with his short blond hair and sparkling blue eyes had cornered me after lunch, hitting on me so hard I was dazzled. Or maybe bedazzled by those sparkling teeth.

No guy had ever hit on me like that. Heck, no guy had ever *looked* at me like that. I felt all warm and fuzzy just thinking about that look.

Margo's eyes were so wide by the time I finished, it looked a little painful.

That was what I'd set out to accomplish and so far I'd succeeded. I'd done it.

For one day. Now I just had to do it again every day of the year. No pressure.

"Are you going to go out with him?" Margo asked.

I shrugged. He hadn't actually asked me out. He'd just called me "beautiful" a lot and gave me a look that said he'd like to order me for dessert.

"He didn't ask," I said.

"He will." Trent didn't look amused, and he didn't seem pleased as his gaze moved over me again. All those guys were eyeing me like I was sex on a stick but my best friend looked at me like I was meat that had gone rotten. "Trust me, he will."

HE DID. Trent was right. Alex asked me out exactly one week later. I was on my way out of the cafeteria and he caught me by surprise. "Hey, beautiful." He jogged to catch up with me. "You didn't sit with me at lunch today."

I blinked over at him. *Great observation, Einstein.* Of course, I didn't say that. That was what old me would have said. And so would begin the kind of sarcastic, teasing, tousle my hair like I'm his little brother type friendship that I was used to with the guys back at my old school. So instead I tucked some hair behind my ear and wondered for the millionth time how girls managed to keep their hair down without going insane.

Was it just my hair that constantly fell into my face? But Margo assured me that my hair down and blown out in pretty, beach-waves-that-look-effortless-but-totally-aren't softened my face. Whatever the hell that means. I have no idea. I just take her word for it.

He seemed to be waiting for a response. "Nope, not today."

Because there's nothing I love more than stating the obvious. I'd never sat with Alex. I always sat with Melody and her friends. Why? Well, because Melody was nice to me, but also because Alex always sat with Drew and I had been going out of my way to stay away from him.

He grinned and those pearly white teeth flashed against his tanned skin. "How about tomorrow?"

I opened my mouth, hoping a good excuse would come to me. "Um…" Thanks to Drew, I couldn't sit with Alex, even if I wanted to.

And I did want to. Alex seemed sweet and funny, and have I mentioned how hot he was? But he was also friends with Drew and I was determined to keep my distance. I'd managed to avoid talking to Drew—or running smack into him—for an entire week, but sitting with him and his friends at lunch would be tempting fate. He didn't remember me, and I was embracing that fact.

Good. Good riddance. Who needed him to remember that we used to eat glue together? Not me.

But now I was stumped on an excuse for why I wouldn't join Alex for lunch. I mean, Melody and her friends were nice and all, but it wasn't like I'd signed some oath that required me to eat there every day.

Alex gave me an excuse. "It's Tina, right?"

I stared at him. Tina? I assumed he meant Tina Withers, who I'd met in passing. She was a friend of Melody's but didn't have the same lunch schedule as us. Tina was petite, blonde, and a cheerleader, and that was about all I knew of her. She'd been nice enough to me when I met her, but that was the extent of my knowledge, so I found myself saying, "Umm..."

He grinned again, like we were in on some secret. "No worries, beautiful. If you can't have lunch with me, then what do you say I take you out for dinner?"

I stared at him. I couldn't help it. Much as I might have prepared for this moment—nothing could have prepared me for this moment. A guy was asking me out. A hot, popular, nice guy was asking me out.

And not as a joke.

He was legit asking me out. I realize I'm belaboring the point, but seriously... this was so surreal. Like maybe whales would start swimming down the hallway on a tide of balloons kind of surreal.

Things like this just did not happen to me.

"Yeah, okay," I managed. I tried to sound cool and laid back but I'm pretty sure it came out as a squeak.

And then Drew Remi ruined everything, because apparently that was his role in life. Drew Remi, ladies and gentlemen, my very own ruiner of everything.

"Hey." He gave Alex a very manly jerk of his chin as he walked up to us. Then he turned to me. "Hi, Veronica."

I did what I've done every time I was forced to be in close contact to Drew. I ducked my head, letting my hair act as a curtain as I mumbled a hello. It seemed this hair-in-face torture served one purpose, at least.

I turned, ready to make my retreat, but apparently Alex wasn't done with our conversation because he slung an arm around my shoulders as he greeted Drew like he was some long lost prodigal son. But then, Alex seemed to greet everyone that way. He was a nice guy. And now Melody and her friend Angela were coming up to us and I couldn't run away without looking like I was... well, running away.

All of us walked in a slow clump that rudely took up the whole hallway. "You coming to watch our practice after school?"

Alex's words lingered for a bit too long and I looked up in surprise to see that he was talking to me. So many of those things took me by surprise I didn't even know how to respond.

I knew that their baseball team was good. Like, probably heading-to-state good. But I couldn't imagine why he'd think I'd want to go and watch them practice. I mean, a game? Sure. I loved going to games, but practice? Why would I want to watch them practice? I had my own practice to go to.

"Um..." I hadn't quite figured out how to say any of that, but Melody answered for me.

"She doesn't have to go to your practice if she doesn't want to, Alex."

Of course I didn't have to go. There was something in her tone that threw me, like she was trying to tell him something.

But then her friend cut in. "Yeah, maybe she's not into sports."

I was. Obviously. But they didn't know that and for a moment I reveled in my anonymity. In the fact that for once in my life I could be anything or anyone. I could be super smart or really into musicals or maybe chess was my thing. They didn't know. All they knew was what I told them and how I acted.

"You don't like sports?" Drew asked. He sounded put out. Why? I couldn't imagine. I'd barely spoken to him this whole past week and when I did it was in mumbles.

Even now I shrugged and managed a mumbled, "Umm..." before Melody answered for me again. "What do you care, Drew? I thought you didn't like it when we came to practices."

I glanced over at him through my curtain of hair, waiting for his response.

He gave Melody an easy smile. "I just like to stay focused, that's all. And who could focus with you ladies around?"

Ugh. I almost made a gagging sound but stopped myself right in time. But seriously, this sounded like a scene from the 50s or something. The guys got to have all the fun while the girls could sit around and swoon at their bulging muscles and tight butts. I bet in Drew's mind we were all cheerleaders who lived to wave our pom-poms at the big game.

Um, I don't think so. I was all for cheerleading—I had enough friends who were cheerleaders to know that it took some serious gymnastic skills, but that wasn't the only area where girls could shine. *Some of us have games of our own to practice for,* I wanted to say. *Some of us have a life.*

Melody made a pouty face at Drew that did nothing for my gag reflexes. *Do not roll your eyes*, I commanded. *Do not do it.*

"Don't give the new girl a hard time just because she's not into watching you," Melody said.

Somehow, but I'm not sure exactly how, I got the feeling that I was being insulted. Not outright insulted, but like I was being... undercut. Maybe it was because she'd called me "new girl" instead of my name. But if felt like what she was really saying was, *Don't blame Veronica for being lame.*

Or maybe I was just paranoid.

Alex jumped back into the conversation, saving me from any more paranoid thoughts. "Why wouldn't she want to watch me in action?" He pretended to preen, making the rest of us laugh. He leaned in so he was talking directly into my ear. "Trust me, I look good out there."

I laughed along with the others but I was superbly conscious of how close he was. I wasn't used to this kind of physical intimacy with a guy, even if he had just asked me out, and I definitely wasn't used to PDA.

I could feel heat in my cheeks as I cast a glance at the others. Melody and her friend were rolling their eyes. Drew was shaking his head, but he was smiling too.

Man, he had a really nice smile.

"You look good because I make you look good," Drew said.

Alex laughed and the two started ripping on each other in a way that felt oddly familiar. They might be popular and they might be at a private school, but they sounded just like all teammates everywhere.

This was what I'd missed since coming to Briarwood. Well, not *this*, but my teammates' version of this. The bond that comes with working hard toward a common goal. Thankfully soccer practice started up after school today. I might not know my teammates yet, but I knew without a doubt that I would find a place to belong on the team. It might not be *all* I am, but a team player is a big part of who I am.

The group of us reached the end of the hall and it was time to split up and go our different ways. Alex squeezed my shoulder. "See you Friday."

I nodded and gave him a shy smile, even though I was thinking, *I'll also see you later today and tomorrow and every day between now and then.*

But I kept quiet. Because I had a date.

My first date. That's right, my first date. Ever. So yeah, maybe now you can see why I needed an image overhaul. I'd been lost in the land of the dateless back at Atwater, but here? One week in and I was going out with one of the school's most eligible bachelors.

I headed down the south hallway, ready to revel in my excitement, thinking of how exactly I was going to spill this news to Margo and Trent. Well, Margo mainly. Trent would roll his eyes. But Margo would be psyched and—

"So, you don't like sports."

I jumped at the sound of Drew's voice next to me. I was on the tall side but he was taller and I felt like he was looming over me in his attempt to walk by my side through the crowded hallway.

Dammit, I'd been caught by the enemy!

In my head I'd started thinking of him as the enemy. He might not know it, but that's kind of what he was. Why? Because he was the only person in this school who could ruin everything for me. Again, my own personal ruiner of everything. The name fit.

I tried to focus on what he'd said. Clearly he wanted to prolong that conversation, just the two of us.

Neat.

I shrugged, quickening my pace. "Um, not really."

Crap, I hadn't wanted to actually outright lie, but what could I do? His gaze was on my face, and I could feel the weight of his stare. If he connected me to sports, he'd recognize me. Maybe.

Unless I was that completely and utterly forgettable. Jeez, what a depressing thought.

"Look," he started.

I picked up my pace even more—the door to my next classroom was in sight. If I could just get there, I could end this conversation before it went any further.

He startled me with a laugh. It wasn't a funny "ha ha" laugh. It was a rueful laugh, almost self-deprecating. "Look," he said again. "You don't have to run away from me."

I instantly slowed down, my cheeks burning up under his scrutiny, a sensation that was neither pleasant nor familiar. I didn't turn to face him, but I didn't ignore him either, defensiveness winning out over my fear of being remembered and my anger at not being remembered.

Clearly my feelings around Drew were complicated.

"I'm not running," I said.

He laughed again. "If that's not you running, you should definitely try out for track."

I couldn't help it. I laughed. I had this image of me with my pretty makeup and my insanely time-consuming beach waves running through a finish line as I headed into Mrs. Olang's geometry class.

I glanced over at him and saw that he was grinning, clearly pleased that I'd laughed.

It was cute, really. His grin was boyish and charming, not that sexy smirk I usually saw on his face. This one reminded me of the boy who used to play touch football with me at recess back in the day.

My smile fell as soon as I remembered our shared past.

His smile faded too and he scratched the back of his neck in a rare display of discomfort. "I've gotta ask. Did I do something wrong?"

I snapped my attention back to the door down the hallway. If I took off now, I could be through those doors and far away from this awkward moment in about three seconds.

"No, of course not," I said quickly, automatically. My innate politeness refused to let me say anything else. Besides, what could I say?

I hate what you represent. I hate the way you and your friends made me feel from junior high on. I hate that I can't forget who I used to be when you're around. I hate that you don't remember me or recognize me... or maybe both. I hate that you're still hot and popular and that it all comes so easily to you.

No, I couldn't say any of that. Instead, I said nothing.

After an epically awkward pause, he let out a huff of a laugh. "Okay, so...what? You just don't like me?"

"No!" What kind of horrible blunt question was that? Besides, what did he care?

And then it dawned on me. It must be a blow to his pride. From what I could tell, every girl and her sister had a thing for him, whether they openly admitted it or not.

Take Melody for example. She said they were just friends but I saw the way she acted around him, the way she watched him. So obvious. She'd even warned me off him on my second day. She'd caught me sneaking a peek in his direction and had said, "Don't bother. Drew doesn't date." I'd looked to her in surprise and found her smirking at me. I didn't ask why. I guess I hadn't wanted Melody or any of the others to think I shared their interest. As far as I was concerned, he was all theirs.

But that must be why it bugged him, and it clearly bugged him. Why else would he ask me like that?

And had I really been *that* rude?

Yes. The answer was yes. The thing was, I didn't think

he'd really notice or care. I mean, he wouldn't have if it had been Ronnie ignoring him. If we were back at our old school, and I was back in my comfortable clothes and my bushy ponytail and my makeup-less face, he wouldn't have even noticed I was alive, let alone cared that I wasn't responding to his jokes.

But you're not back at your old school, I reminded myself. And he was still waiting for some sort of explanation, even though I couldn't figure out why it mattered.

I licked my lips as I tried to come up with a good explanation. "It's not that I don't like you, it's just..." I held my breath hoping that inspiration would hit. My mind raced with conversations we'd had in group settings, something that would explain my lack of interest, if not my rudeness. Every conversation I could remember was eerily similar to the one we'd just left behind, all of which seemed to revolve around their baseball team, which was on its way to playoffs.

I blurted it out before I could think it through. "I just don't like athletes, that's all."

The moment it was out, I realized how dumb it sounded. Also, there was a very obvious flaw in that logic.

His brow furrowed in disbelief. "Didn't you just agree to go out with Alex?"

Um... yes? Crap.

But also, why did he look so bent out of shape about that? I thought he and Alex were friends.

I shook off the thought. I could overanalyze later with Margo and Trent.

I pictured Trent's look of disgust whenever the topic of boys came up. Okay fine, I'd analyze later with Margo. For now, I had an awkward encounter to escape and a class to get to. I started backing away, heading toward my classroom as I gave him a little shrug. "Sorry. I didn't mean to be rude or anything, it's just...." I shrugged again. "Alex is the exception, I guess."

He nodded. "Yeah, I guess."

What did that mean? "Sports, athletes, jocks..." I rambled as I backed away. "Just not my thing." I thought of Alex and I'm pretty sure Drew was thinking the same thing as he arched a brow.

"Normally, I mean."

He nodded again, and this time I could have sworn his smile was taunting me. "Sure."

I whirled around and bolted into the classroom, my heart racing as I found my seat and cracked my book, pretending to be absorbed by the problems that swam in front of my eyes.

I was only one week in but suddenly everything felt too complicated. The date that I'd been so excited about made me anxious. What would we talk about? What was I supposed to wear? I was doubting the new friends I'd been so excited about. Why had Melody talked about me like I wasn't there? Why was she calling me "the new girl" like I didn't have a name?

Relax, Ronnie. I focused on my breathing as the other students slid into their seats. I was spiraling into paranoia-land and it was ridiculous. I was getting everything I ever wanted. A hot, popular guy wanted to date me. I had friends who were the popular girls... Heck, even Drew Remi finally noticed me.

But that thought made my chest tighten and breathing seemed impossible. Drew was at the heart of all these new problems. If he wasn't here I'd be fine. But every time he was near he made it impossible to forget who I used to be.

When he was around I felt like a fake. A fraud.

But I wasn't, I reminded myself. This was me, just with better hair, makeup and clothes. It didn't change who I really was. I was still me, just better.

Guilt and shame rose up like a tidal wave as I remembered my desperate words of parting. The outright lie about not liking athletes.

How could I not like athletes? I *was* an athlete, and a damned good one.

The teacher walked to the front of the room and I focused all my attention on her, grateful to have something other than my own thoughts to fixate on. Quite frankly, my thoughts were making me uncomfortable in my own skin.

All of Trent's judgements and criticisms came back to haunt me. I'd told him over and over again that by being this new version of me I wasn't denying who I was, I wasn't trying to be someone different. So what was that back there?

It was Drew Remi's fault, all of it. I'd never meant to lie. I shouldn't have had to.

It was official. Drew Remi was ruining everything.

I watched the teacher talk but realized I hadn't caught anything she'd said for the past five minutes. My mind kept insisting on replaying my parting words and the feeling of shame grew with each passing second. Much as I wanted to be angry at Drew, I couldn't fool myself.

It wasn't Drew who'd ruined everything in that moment... that was all me.

FOUR

Drew

I THREW another pitch and watched as it veered wildly. I don't know what I'd been thinking. I *hadn't* been thinking.

The catcher scrambled to catch my failed pitch. Damn, I was off my game today. I'd been off my game all practice and there was one reason why. Veronica Smith. I couldn't stop replaying what she'd said, what I'd said, what she'd meant, what I'd thought.

Ugh. I was boring myself.

Except that I wasn't. For days now Veronica had been front and center in my mind. The topic of Veronica seemed to be endlessly fascinating to some part of my brain. A part of my brain that I couldn't control. It was also the part of my brain that couldn't care less about the playoffs, apparently.

It was beyond frustrating. Ever since the whole April disaster last year, I'd sworn off dating. I mean, hookups were one thing, but the last thing I needed was another chick messing with my head.

I had enough going on in my life without getting all twisted out of shape over a girl who I'd probably never see again once I went off to college. High school relationships didn't last. Just ask my parents.

Of course, they'd had two kids and a seventeen-year marriage before they came to that realization but I figure I'd learn from their lesson. Watching their marriage fall apart was all the lesson I'd ever need in why young love didn't last. My parents may have been in love at some point, but no longer. They might have been friends once, and maybe they'd even had something in common, but these days that was hard to imagine.

And if my parents hadn't made it clear that high school relationships were doomed to fail, April had driven the point home. We'd been going out for more than a year when I'd left. By the way she'd carried on when I'd said I was leaving for California, you would have thought her world was ending. We'd agreed to try the long distance thing, mainly because I'd hated to see her cry, but also because everything in my life was falling apart and having one consistent relationship had been appealing.

I should have known April couldn't do long distance. Our relationship had barely survived at Atwater, where we had all the same friends and saw each other every single day. Honestly I'd thought that was part of our problem. We saw each other all the time and her tendency to gossip and stir up drama had driven me crazy. I'd honestly thought that maybe long distance would work for us.

But then, less than two weeks after my move to California, I found out that she'd started seeing my former friend and teammate, Lee. She hadn't told me, I'd seen pictures on Instagram.

Yup, social media. That's exactly how a guy wants to find out he's been dumped.

Part of me wondered if she'd regretted her decision when I ended up moving back before the school year was even over. I could have gone back to Atwater, but my parents gave me a choice. We all knew the Briarwood team was better and they wanted me. Maybe if things hadn't gone so badly with April and my other friends at Atwater I would have opted for a lifetime of friendships over baseball. But between the better team and a chance to start fresh without the drama and mind games, Briarwood had been too tempting to pass up.

I threw another ball, hitting my target perfectly this time, and some of my anxiety eased up. Maybe I wasn't so far off my game after all. And maybe my ex and my former friends had done me a favor.

I'd learned my lesson and had cut out girl drama. All of my attention was on my game these days, and that laser focus had helped take our team to playoffs. Life was so much easier now that the family tension had died down and my social life consisted of baseball and hookups. No close friendships and no girlfriends. Life was so much simpler this way.

Besides, I had to focus on baseball if I wanted to get into a good school. My mom was depending on me to get a scholarship to college, and I wanted that too. I wasn't a bad student but I didn't have amazing grades, so I needed this.

Not to mention, I wanted to win.

With that thought I focused on the ball in my hand, forcibly blocking out all thoughts of a tall, sexy, mystery girl named Veronica.

Thwack.

Thank goodness. I let my head fall back in relief.

Tomorrow night was our next game and I couldn't afford to fall into a losing streak now. My team was depending on me and I needed this win.

I don't like sports.

Her words rang in my head making me furious for some reason I couldn't quite figure out. Who cared if she was into sports or athletes?

I do.

But I shouldn't. Obviously we don't have much in common if she turned her nose up baseball. I live and breathe this sport.

This was a good thing, I decided. If she was one of those girls who was too girlie to break a sweat or couldn't find anything interesting in a game that required skill and dedication, then I was better off not getting close. It wasn't like I was looking for a relationship, anyways, and this just helped rule out temptation.

I stared down at the ball in his hand. Why did that mental pep talk do nothing to make me feel better?

Probably because I had an image of her in my head that I couldn't shake. It was the way she'd smiled at Alex. It was that little smile she'd given me for a half a second when I'd teased her about trying out for track.

That smile had slayed me. I don't even remember having a moment like that with April and we'd been together for ages. It wasn't just the smile; it was the connection.

And yeah, it had only lasted for a heartbeat, but in that moment life had come to a stop. Kind of like that moment when her eyes had met mine when she'd fallen into my arms.

There was something familiar about her, like I'd known her in another lifetime. Her smile made me want to hear her laugh—not the polite little giggles I'd heard when she was talking to Alex, but a genuine laugh.

I wanted to be the one who made her laugh. I wanted it so badly it hurt.

I wanted to hang out with her and talk with her. The closest I'd gotten was eavesdropping on her conversations with Alex. I'd heard enough to know that I loved her voice, kind of husky and sexy as hell. I'd heard her joking with one of our classmates in English Lit the other day and her humor had been teasing but warm. In that moment I'd desperately wanted to be her friend.

That sounds weird, but it's true. I'd lost a lot of my close friends when I'd left Atwater. No, that's not true. I lost them when I found out that April had moved on to my friend before I'd even unpacked in California and neither of them had the decency to tell me.

Ever since I'd come back to town I'd managed to avoid them and all our other friends. Word spread that I was back at Briarwood, but I'd made excuses about having to catch up on schoolwork and needing to hang out with my new teammates.

I don't think anyone bought it. It was probably totally obvious that I was just avoiding running into April and Lee. And I had been avoiding—I'd unfriended them on Facebook, stopped following them on Instagram and SnapChat. I didn't want to know about the drama going on without me. Though I had a feeling April and Lee weren't together anymore. How did I know?

She'd been texting. Cute little friendly messages at first that I probably should have ignored, but I hadn't wanted to get into a fight with her. April was tough to navigate like that. If I was outright rude, she'd take it as a cue to start fighting with me. If I was too nice, she'd think I wanted to get back together. So I'd replied just often enough to avoid being rude, but not too much to give her any ideas.

But lately her texts had been more forward, asking if I wanted to get together, inviting me to parties. No mention of Lee or any other guys. I knew her well enough to know what was going on, but I wanted no part of those games anymore.

But all that being said, I'd be lying if I said I didn't miss having friends. I mean, I had my teammates at Briarwood but I didn't have any good friends, not ones I could talk to about my messed up home life.

Why did I think Veronica would be a good friend? I don't know, I just did. There was something warm and real about her. And she seemed... nice.

To everyone except me, of course.

I threw the ball so hard the catcher cursed as he caught it.

Maybe that's why I was so obsessed. The fact that I'd been singled out for this rude treatment—that would be enough to drive anyone crazy. The thought calmed me a bit. Yeah, that had to be it. I'm not crazy egotistical or anything but I'm a normal male and I have an ego. Of course it was going to suck when the new hot chick looked at you like you're a leper. And sure, it stung that she liked Alex even though her whole excuse for treating me like a creeper was because I'm into sports.

So she didn't like athletes—which was weird on its own—but she liked *Alex*? He was about as stereotypical as one could get. He was a total jock who lived for sports. His grades sucked and his conversations almost exclusively revolved around the latest game for whatever season we happened to be in. And football had just started, which was his favorite. Actually, it was messing with our playoff run for the summer league, which was pissing me off.

I mean, don't get me wrong. I liked the guy but he wasn't exactly deep.

The shallow jock appeared at my side as if I'd called him with my thoughts. "Hey man, you going to the party tomorrow night?"

I didn't answer right away. For some reason Alex's mere presence pissed me off.

"You gotta come, man, it's the first big rager of the school year."

I threw the pitch and once again it veered off course. Damn Alex and his interruptions. He ignored the bad throw and I shook off my irritation. He'd done nothing to deserve my anger.

"I'm taking Veronica," he said.

When I faced him his smile was smug. *I could beat the crap out of this kid.*

Why? He asked out Veronica before I could. Not that she would have said yes, but... Nope. No buts. Even if I'd asked first, she clearly didn't like me, not even as a potential friend, and she obviously liked Alex. I should just get over it already.

That was so much easier said than done when my body felt it like it'd been struck by a weird infatuation version of the flu. Not just my crush on Veronica, but the jealousy that came up every time Alex mentioned her name, the way I couldn't seem to stop thinking about her, the way she'd gotten under my skin...

"Veronica Smith!" He called her name out and I glanced over in shock. How did he know I was thinking about her?

But then I followed his gaze.

No way. No freakin' way.

Veronica, Miss "I hate sports," was clad in soccer attire and she was walking with some teammates across the parking lot. She didn't seem to hear Alex's shout and for a second I was too stunned to say or do much of anything. I just stared.

"Veronica plays soccer?" I stupidly asked.

Alex shrugged. "I guess so."

I tried to tear my gaze away from her, but honestly, it was painful to look away. But then again, it was painful to look at her, too.

She's hot wearing skinny jeans and a T-shirt in the hallways, she's freakin' sexy as hell when she wears skirts and sundresses, but seeing her strutting around in those short shorts that reveal long, toned, tanned legs?

Holy crap, she was breathtaking. Like, literally. I couldn't breathe. Her long brown hair was pulled up in a ponytail that revealed a slender neck and her profile, which was stunning without makeup. She looked so natural, so genuine.

And she looked hot.

The catcher had walked over to us at some point and I heard him whistle. "Dude, you are so lucky."

That finally broke the spell because I realized that he wasn't talking to me. He was talking to Alex.

Alex, the uber jock, who for some unknown reason was taking Veronica to a party.

"You're taking Veronica," I said, repeating his earlier words.

His grin made me want to shove my fist into his throat. "Yeah, man. Don't be jealous just because your favorite outfielder's got game."

"Won't Tina be at the party?" I asked.

Alex's grin turned knowing. "Of course. Why do you think I'm bringing the hot new girl?"

The hot new girl. He didn't even use her name. Rage boiled up inside me. Alex was just using Veronica to get to Tina. I might not have been at Briarwood for a while but it hadn't taken long to figure those two out. On-again-off-again and addicted to their little mind games.

Just like me and April.

I shuddered at the thought. But now wasn't the time to worry about the past. Veronica might not be nice to me but she seemed like a good person. And she was the new girl. Alex was exploiting both of those traits by turning her into his unwitting accomplice.

I had to tell her. Without really thinking it through, I turned to chase after her.

"Where are you going?" Alex asked.

"I need to talk to Veronica about something," he said.

Alex laughed behind me. "Dude, give it up. She doesn't like you."

I ignored him and his laughter.

He was right. She didn't like me, and that sucked. But that didn't mean I shouldn't help her out. One new kid to another.

That's what I told myself as I chased her down. This wasn't a pathetic attempt to squash her date with Alex. Nope. I wasn't *that* jealous.

Lie. Lie. Lie.

"Veronica, wait up!"

She came to a stop and I watched her expression register shock and then... horror.

Jeez, what had I ever done to her?

Before I could ask, a car pulled up beside her and she

said something to the girl she was talking to before jumping into the Prius like it was her getaway car.

A guy was driving, but I couldn't make him out. The girl she'd been talking to—the one from the soccer team—looked back at me in confusion.

Okay, so at least I wasn't the only one who'd seen it. She'd looked terrified at the sight of me. Or maybe just horrified. Neither was terribly good for my ego.

Hell, I just wanted to be her friend. My mind helpfully called up an image of those long lean legs in those itty-bitty shorts. Fine, maybe I'd prefer to be more than friends. But I'd settle for friends.

At this point, I'd settle for an honest answer to the question—what had I done wrong? Why was I the only person in school who got the cold shoulder instead of that sunny smile?

I wasn't sure how long I stood there, obsessing for the millionth time even though I'd just promised myself I'd let go of this particular line of thought. But then a car honking next to me pulled me out of my funk.

My little sister, Eloise, was behind the wheel of the beater we shared. Our parents hadn't been able to afford a new car for one kid, let alone two of us, and now that me and El were both of age to drive, we'd decided to go in on one together.

Unfortunately this clunker was all we'd been able to afford between our part-time summer jobs and birthday money.

El gave me a little wave. It still felt weird to see my little sister driving. Maybe everyone else in the world saw her as a mature sixteen-year-old sophomore, but in my mind she would always be a little kid.

The little kid in question waved again, clearly losing

patience that I was keeping her waiting. All around me my teammates were piling into cars or getting into their rides.

Crap. I'd wasted an entire practice on the great mystery that was Veronica Smith.

I muttered a curse as I slid into the passenger side. I half expected El to give me a hard time about making her wait but she was squinting at the empty spot ahead of us where Veronica had dove into that car.

"You didn't tell me Ronnie Smith transferred to Briarwood."

I stared at her.

Ronnie Smith. Ronnie Smith. Ronnie—the name clicked into place, finding the context in my memories.

I was too stunned to talk. Too shocked to breathe. I stared at the empty space too. No, it couldn't be.

Ronnie. Veronica. Was Ronnie a nickname for Veronica? How had I never known that?

I shook my head. Really? That was the detail my brain focused on? I tried to summon up a mental image of Ronnie. Ronnie Smith, as in the tomboy who'd been in my class forever. The one who'd played with all the boys when she was younger and then, as she'd gotten older... I struggled to remember what happened to her when she'd gotten older.

My mental image of her was fuzzy, but it didn't gel with Veronica Smith, the hot new student. It was like trying to mesh together two puzzle pieces that just didn't fit. The result was a fuzzy mishmash.

"You didn't recognize her?" El asked. There was laughter in her voice. Like this was funny. As if this was a joke.

I groaned as I dropped my head into my hands. That was Ronnie freakin' Smith. Veronica Smith was Ronnie. Holy crap, how had I been so blind? No wonder she hated me. How could I have failed to recognize her? We'd known each other forever. She must think I was the worst sort of self-absorbed jerk.

But then again, she didn't look like Ronnie—not the Ronnie I remembered, at least. She looked so different, so grown up, so...hot.

A new realization had me sitting up straight. Oh man. I'd been fantasizing over *Ronnie*.

That was just too weird. I'd gone to grade school with Ronnie. I'd learned how to swing a bat alongside Ronnie at recess. We used to race each other at the local pool. And now I was fantasizing about her?

El pulled out of the parking lot, but if she was talking I couldn't hear her. Those two names kept racing through my mind in an endless loop as I tried to wrap my head around the fact that they were one in the same person.

Veronica was Ronnie.

My mind was officially blown.

FIVE

Veronica

TRENT KEPT GLANCING at me out of the corner of his eye. "Why do you look so freaked, Ron?"

"I'm not freaked." *Liar, liar, pants on fire.* I'm so freaked. Ever since that awful run-in with Drew in the hall, I'd been scared of seeing him again.

Now it wasn't just that I didn't want him to figure out who I really am. Now it was so much more. I was afraid he'd see straight through my lies, I was afraid he'd look into my eyes and see, oh I don't know—everything.

Today it had finally happened. After days of avoiding him, he'd not only tracked me down, he'd caught me coming from soccer practice.

Soccer.

AKA a sport.

I groaned as I slid down further into the car's seats. "I've made such a mess of this." I looked over to see Trent grinning as he watched the road. "I'm so glad my tragedy amuses you."

He glanced over, not even trying to hide his smile. "It's not too late to transfer back."

I snorted. "And admit defeat after two weeks?" I gave him a sidelong glare. "I don't think so."

"There's my girl," he said, patting my knee condescendingly enough that I felt required to smack his shoulder. Hard.

"Ow." He rubbed it, giving me that kicked puppy dog look that never failed to make me feel bad. "I was just trying to give you a pep talk."

Rolling my eyes, I smacked him again, a little less hard this time. "Oh please. You're being a condescending ass."

He cast me a sidelong look and I let out a little laugh. "Okay, yeah. Maybe I deserve it. I suppose I've been acting a little crazy lately."

"Crazy's one way of putting it." My best friend since birth pretended to toss his non-existent long hair and donned the worst Valley Girl accent I'd ever heard. "Oh. My. Gaaawwd. The boy I like likes me back and the other boy I like doesn't know that I like him and he doesn't know who I am but, like, I think that I like that but maybe I don't and—Ow!"

I'd smacked his shoulder so hard the sound seemed to echo in the car. "Sorry." Not really, he'd had it coming. I tried not to laugh. I mean, he *was* making fun of me and I didn't want to reward him by laughing.

But I couldn't help it. I let my head fall back as the last of my carefully constructed image faded away like a bad dye job. It felt good to laugh like an idiot, snorts and all. It was a relief to have my feet up on his dash and be sporting my sweaty soccer uniform.

"You've got to admit," Trent said. "I have a point."

I sobered at that. "Yeah, I know you do. And you deserve a medal of honor for putting up with my craziness these last couple weeks. You and Margo both."

He let out a loud laugh. "Margo? Are you kidding? She's having a field day with all... this." He waved his hand in a dismissive gesture toward my hair and face. *This*, apparently, meant the new and improved "best version of me" that Margo had created and helped maintain. If it weren't for her, I might have fallen off the blowout wagon a week ago.

"She's been great," I said, watching and loving as his mouth twisted up in a cute little smirk.

Trent might not be the most emotive guy on the planet but for anyone who knew him well, it was totally obvious that he was head over heels for his sweetheart of a girlfriend. My secret glee over Trent's sappiness was almost instantly replaced with a pang.

That. That was what I wanted. The kind of connection they had, the excitement of dating and relationships. That was the whole reason I'd wanted to do this whole "new and improved" Veronica routine. I stared ahead at the road. I just had to stay focused on my goal and not worry about everything else.

Like Drew. Or the fact that he'd seen me in my soccer outfit today, which pretty clearly confirmed that I was a big fat liar who loved to lie. I didn't even realize I'd groaned until Trent looked over again. "Okay, spill."

I shook my head. "You don't want to hear it, and I don't want to talk about it."

This was the truth. I was so tired of thinking about Drew Remi, the last thing I wanted was to talk about him. Besides, I already knew what Trent would say.

You're being an idiot.

And he'd be right. I should never have lied in the first place. And by lie I mean the lie of omission I'd started by pretending that I also didn't know who he was. This whole situation was ludicrous. At some point he would figure out who I really was or he'd out me to his friends as the psycho sports-loving liar I've been these last two weeks.

Either way, one of the hottest and most popular guys at Briarwood had all the ammunition necessary to put a definitive end to the great *Veronica* 2.0 experiment.

I held back another groan of self pity.

But, I reminded myself, all Drew issues aside, this whole plan was going well. I mean, I had a date. My first date. Which could very possibly lead to my first kiss.

I glanced over at Trent. Nope. No way he'd be cool chatting about kissing and dating. Better wait until I saw Margo.

Margo would know what I should wear to the party. She'd know what I should talk about at dinner with Alex. The thought of Alex made me remember a moment at the end of practice I'd almost forgotten. One of the girls had made a weird comment about him and Tina and—

"Earth to Ronnie." Trent was using his stupid robot voice, which had been lame when we were kids and had not gotten cooler as he'd aged.

"Sorry, what did you say?"

He gave me a funny look but let it go. "I said the guys are coming over, you want to hang out?"

"The guys" meant our friends, Pete, Robbie, and Luke. It was always the same group and "hang out" meant eating pizza and playing video games until we were either ready to puke from too much cheese or pass out in a carb coma.

I sighed as I thought about all the primping and prodding that would come tomorrow as I once again slipped into my new Margo-approved clothes and played the role of normal teenage girl.

"Honestly? That sounds like heaven right now."

And it was. A little while later I was firmly entrenched on the couch in Trent's basement, playing a game I'd played a million times before and listening to my friends talk smack like they'd done a million times before.

They caught me up on the gossip at my old school—not the girlie gossip, but the funny stuff. Like how old Mrs. Haggerty had finally gotten her dream come true and left to tape an episode of *Wheel of Fortune* last week. And how no one could figure out who specifically had hacked into the teacher's online forum so they'd brought in every single student who'd logged in to the computer lab that week.

The conversation was easy, the pizza greasy, and all thoughts of Drew Remi or any other Briarwood drama was temporarily put on hold.

All in all, that night was perfection.

THE NEXT NIGHT, on the other hand...

"You cannot be serious." I glared at Margo in my bedroom mirror.

She held up an eyelash curler and arched one brow. "Do I look like I'm kidding?"

I pursed my lips but then let out a sigh. "In for a penny, in for a pound."

"What does that mean?" she asked. Now she was the one frowning as she came toward me with that metal torture device.

"I have no idea," I said. "It sounds good though."

She made a *mmm* noise that I took as agreement, though she'd clearly lost interest as her attention was avidly focused on my eyes. Which was good. If someone was going to perform minor surgery to my eyelashes, I hoped they'd be focused.

"You are going to look sooo hot," she murmured. "Drew Remi is not even going to recognize you."

I gave a little snort of amusement. "Funny."

She grinned down at me as she leaned back to assess her handiwork on eye number one. "I thought so."

"It's not Drew I need to impress though," I said. I shifted a little but as she was once again coming at me with the metal wand, I stopped and froze.

"That's right. So tell me about this Alex guy," she said.

I told her everything I knew, which, to be honest, wasn't a whole lot. In my defense, I'd only been going to school with this guy for two weeks and we had no classes together so all the info I had was from our little tête-à-têtes outside the cafeteria and our short walks together down the hall.

"He sounds nice," she said.

I nodded. Yeah, nice. Such a bland word and not one that really captured Alex, but I didn't have a better description. Besides, I'd become more focused on what my teammate had said after soccer practice the other day.

I'd mentioned that he was taking me to Melody's party and she'd given me this weird look. "Alex," she'd repeated. And then, "Alex Wilson?"

I'd nodded. We were definitely talking about the same Alex. But then she'd said, "Tina's Alex?"

I'd wanted to ask her what she'd meant by that but then Drew had shouted out my name and I'd done what I now seem to do best whenever my old friend was around. I panicked, diving into Trent's car and temporarily forgetting all about that weird remark.

I'd managed to block it out until now. Now when I had approximately twenty minutes until he was set to pick me up.

I don't know why I thought Margo would know, but she was so much better at the whole dealing with high school girls thing so I told her everything as she helped me get ready.

Now she was frowning at me, her brows drawn together in consternation. "I don't like the sound of that."

I arched my brows. "Join the club."

Margo sank beside me on the bench seat we'd pulled into my bedroom for makeover sessions. "Maybe Tina and Alex were a couple and they just broke up."

I shrugged. "Maybe." It was as good a guess as any. "I mean, they can't still be together, right? He wouldn't ask me out if he had a girlfriend."

Even to my own ears it sounded like I was trying to convince myself.

She nodded hesitantly. "Yeah. Right."

"And it's not a secret. Melody and Drew and some others heard him talking to me about it, so…."

She nodded with a little more enthusiasm, which eased some of my tension. "Yeah, totally. She's probably his ex or something." She gave me a forced smile. "You'll just have to feel it out at the party, I guess. But don't worry. Even if you're stepping on some other girl's toes, you've got the excuse of being the new girl."

The anxious feeling came back with a vengeance. First of all, Tina was not just "some girl." I barely knew her but I knew that much about her. She had the kind of cool, ringleader vibe that April had in our old school. There were some girls who just seemed to have that quality. They were natural leaders.

Or maybe they were just naturally intimidating. Either way, I did not have that quality and neither did Margo.

She was watching me now with such hopeful optimistic eyes I could only smile and nod. "You're right. It will totally be fine."

Spoiler alert. It was not fine. Not even a little bit fine.

The whole "date" was a disaster. And I'm using quotes for a reason. I know I had no experience with dating but whatever that was with Alex, it so did not qualify as a date in my books.

First of all, there was no dinner. He honked the horn and I went out to meet him—no, I didn't expect a corsage and roses, but seriously. Getting honked at like I'm late for carpool? Not exactly the most flattering way to start off my first date.

Then when I got in he grinned, told me I looked hot, and also informed me that he ate already so let's just get to the party.

I had not eaten. Why would I have eaten when I'd thought we were going out to eat? I should have said that. In hindsight I would have told him that. But it all happened so quickly, and I was so nervous, and have I mentioned that this was my first date? Oh yeah, and also my first real high school party. Unless you count our little pizza parties down in Trent's basement, but I'm pretty sure no one would consider those a "party" despite the fact that we down enough pizza to feed an army.

Where was I? Oh right. No food. So there I was, looking "hot" according to Alex, in my short skirt and slinky T-shirt. But I was now starving on top of anxious, and one thought kept playing through my mind. What the hell had my teammate meant by "Tina's Alex?"

I should have asked. In hindsight, I totally would have asked.

I one hundred percent understand that "hindsight is twenty-twenty" saying now. If I could do it all over again, I would.

But I couldn't, so here's what happened. We bypassed dinner and headed straight to the party. Alex wrapped an arm around me and led me to the door. I felt like everything was happening too fast. Not only had we already skipped over a crucial component of this date but everything was happening in warp speed.

Melody's house was close to mine so before I could say "let's change the radio station" we were already pulling up in front of her house. Tons of cars were already there so clearly the party was well underway even though the sun had barely set.

Next thing I knew I was being hustled up the drive as Alex shouted out to people he recognized getting out of a truck nearby.

I didn't recognize them but no one thought to make introductions.

And then we were inside and yet again I felt like I'd skipped something crucial… I mean, other than dinner.

The party must have started early because Melody and all of her friends looked wasted. Have I mentioned that it was dinnertime? I thought parties didn't really get started until later, but what did I know.

Nothing.

Turns out, I knew absolutely nothing. Man, I was so naïve.

"Veronica!" Melody called out, her brown curls

bouncing as she headed over to me and wrapped her arms around my waist. Melody is about half my size so she looked a bit like a child cuddling up to me.

Then she pressed a red plastic cup in my hand and gave me a sloppy grin, her eyes unfocused. "I'm so glad you came."

She sounded so sincere it honestly made me a little weepy. Things had been going well for me at Briarwood, but I could safely say that being the new girl sucked no matter how well I was faking it.

Being new meant there was always an uneasy component to it all. Shifting variables that I could never quite determine. There were always subtexts and hidden agendas, or maybe I was just paranoid? It was impossible to say because unlike at my old school, I didn't know these people, not truly, and I didn't have access to all the information.

A fact that would become appallingly obvious in about... oh, thirty minutes. That was how long it took for Tina to discover that I was there.

And that I'd come with Alex.

For the first half hour or so I hung out in the kitchen with Melody and her friends as Alex came and went. I'd like to say that he kept coming back to the kitchen to check on me, but that would be giving him too much credit.

The kitchen also happened to be where the keg was located and it is with full humility that I admit—as far as my date's priorities were concerned, I came in second to a keg.

I pasted a smile on my face, but the smile hurt. Two weeks of being friendly and acting like I had all the confidence in the world when really I was questioning everything I said and did... It was exhausting. I was tired. I would have paid money to go over to Trent's and join him and the other guys for a round of *Mario Kart*.

I would have sold my soul for a slice of the pizza that they were most likely devouring as I stood there awkwardly pretending to be part of a conversation, even though it was about people I barely knew and their boring lives.

I know, I was being judgy. For a girl who wanted to be playing *Mario Kart* on a Saturday night, I should not be calling other people boring.

But the stories were boring—for me, at least. And the beer was flat and gross. And the kitchen was way too crowded as fellow students of Briarwood continued to file in one after the other.

People were shouting because they were drunk, and then others were shouting to be heard over the people who were originally shouting.

My ears hurt. My cheeks hurt. My stomach hurt.

I was miserable.

And that's when it happened. Alex came in from outside. He sought me out and draped an arm around my shoulders. "How's my favorite date?" he said far too loudly.

I smiled up at him but I'm sure it looked forced. I was having a hard time keeping my lips in the smile formation and I know without a doubt that it didn't reach my eyes.

He didn't seem to notice but I became increasingly aware of the number of eyes focused on me. On us.

Maybe I was being paranoid again. I glanced around and saw Melody peering at us creepily over the rim of her cup. One of her friends leaned in and whispered something to her and they both giggled while still watching me.

Um... okay. That's not weird or anything.

All of the shouting seemed to stop as Tina walked in through the same outside door that Alex had just come through.

The whole thing felt staged. She stopped and stared,

her pretty mouth pursing and her eyes narrowing on Alex's arm around my shoulder.

I knew Alex saw her because his grip tightened on me and the air in the room seemed to grow thicker and heavier. Time seemed to slow as I found myself suddenly and unwittingly part of a scene.

I might be well-rounded but drama has never been my thing. I have no secret desires to be an actress, nor did I want to be in the spotlight. And if I'd ever doubted that decision, this moment confirmed it.

My empty stomach churned so badly I thought I might puke. I looked around frantically for escape from whatever weird high school soap opera I'd just been cast in. But all I saw were stares. Everyone was staring and no one was even pretending otherwise.

Tina stomped over to us, a red paper cup in one hand and the other planted on her hip. Like Melody, Tina was a short, petite little thing. Cute as a button when she wasn't pursing her lips like that, but tiny. So right now, as she came within inches of me, where I couldn't back away thanks to Alex's arm around my shoulders, I was dimly aware of how ridiculous this must look.

I mean, I'm tall and have been kicking butt in soccer since I was five. If I wanted to I could probably take one big step and crush her like a bug. Not that I wanted to, but, you know... I could.

"What are you doing here with *her*?" she sneered. The question was clearly intended for Alex, but she never stopped glaring at me.

The venom in her voice stunned me. I found myself blinking rapidly, trying to figure out what exactly I'd done wrong here. A quick glance around confirmed it. I'd been cast as the hussy harlot in the junior class's production of *Days of our Briarwood*.

What the hell?

"Relax, Tina," Alex said. His tone was bored but I could practically feel his adrenaline pumping, and not with anger.

Oh. My. God. I turned my face up to see him and confirmed my worst suspicions.

He loved this. He loved being the center of attention. He loved being seen as the babe magnet who had two girls fighting over him.

Anger rushed up so swift and fierce it nearly blinded me. He'd done this to me on purpose. I looked over at Melody and her friends. They'd let this happen *on purpose*.

Were they all so freakin' bored that they got their kicks staging these little dramas and ruining a new girl's first date?

No, this would not go down as my first date, I decided right then and there. I had to get out of this situation. I hadn't signed up for this. I tried to wiggle out of his grip as I turned back to Tina and opened my mouth to say, *He's all yours, I don't want him*. But I was stopped by cold, sticky, flat beer thrown in my face and all over my new, Margo-approved T-shirt.

I gasped at the shock of it. Seriously, you try having flat beer thrown in your face and tell me you're not a little stunned. Through it all I heard my gasp echoed by some of the other girls, but those gasps were followed by giggles and whispers and unrestrained glee at my public embarrassment.

My heart started racing and I could hear the blood rushing to my head as anger, hurt, and humiliation waged a war.

Anger won out.

I would crush her like a bug.

I never got the chance. After what felt like a lifetime of shocked silence, everything happened at once. Just as I made a move to strike, I was stopped. Someone blocked my way.

Drew Remi was standing front of me, his back to me as he faced down Tina the Tiny.

"What the hell, Tina," he said, his low voice filled with disgust.

I stared at his back, temporarily stunned silent once more at whatever was unfolding in front of me.

"Get out of my way, Drew." I heard Tina's high-pitched whine. I could imagine her self-righteous haughty pose even though I couldn't see past Drew's back. "That little slut has to learn who she's messing with."

OMG. Seriously? Who wrote the dialogue for this scene and why had they cast me? I was pissed, but more than that, I felt betrayed by these people I'd stupidly thought were my friends.

Alex stood silent next to me but I was dimly aware that he was shaking his head and making a sound of exasperation. If I could translate his sighs, they would be saying something condescending like, *oh silly girls*.

I finally managed to wriggle out from under his arm. I tried to push Drew aside but he was too firmly planted. He didn't seem to notice that I was trying to get around him so I could punch that stupid, adorable button nose, consequences be damned.

If this was what it was like to be part of their inner circle of popularity, I wanted no part of it.

But Drew was all over the situation and I couldn't get a word in edgewise.

"Relax, Tina," he said. His voice still had that tone of lazy amusement, like he couldn't care less about all of this stupid high school crap. His tone was perfect, really. It made everyone else seem immature and melodramatic without him having to outright call them out on it. "Get your facts straight before you go full-on crazy,"

I heard Tina's harsh inhale and knew she was about to retaliate or maybe defend herself. She had to if she wanted to look good for the audience. But Drew didn't give her a chance. He reached back to put his arm around me.

Between him and Alex I was starting to feel like a stuffed animal. Just tuck me under your arm for a quick cuddle.

But with Drew, the half embrace felt nice. Reassuring, even. He might not remember me, but out of all these people he was the only one I truly knew.

And I knew he was a good guy. He'd always stuck up for the underdogs; he'd always taken on the bullies. He was a good guy, whether he'd seen me or not. So I let him pull me up against his side as he stared down at Tina. "I asked Alex to pick Veronica up for me because I couldn't get out of a family dinner in time."

Everyone stared at Drew, including me. We were all absorbing this new twist in the soap opera plotline. I'm pretty sure I looked just as confused as everyone else for half a second there before I realized what he was doing and forced myself to look the part he'd just recast me as.

Drew's date. The poor, sweet new girl who'd been wrongly accused of harlotry by Tina, queen of the mean girls.

It worked. I almost laughed at how well it worked. Tina's haughty expression turned wary. Her glance moved from him to me to Alex. I half expected her to call out "Line!" to someone standing in the wings.

She had clearly not been prepared for this turn of

events. She gathered her wits pretty quickly, to be honest. Whirling around she glared at Alex. "Is this true?"

Alex was born to be an actor. He eased out from behind me and Drew. "Of course, baby." He went to her and the next thing you know, the two of them were making out in the middle of the kitchen.

All that was missing was the swelling music and the rolling credits as the couple everyone was rooting for found their happily ever after.

Again.

Something told me this was not the first nor the last time this couple and their passionate love affair were in the spotlight.

Everyone was happy. The crowd around me went back to talking amongst themselves—about us, no doubt. The key players in an improv scene for the ages.

Alex and Tina went off into a corner where they seemed content to share whispers and caresses. Melody and her friends were laughing about something.

The only person who was not happy? Me.

What the hell was that? Also... I was still wet. And hungry. And angrier than I'd ever been in my entire life.

All of this combined meant I was also dangerously close to tears.

Drew's arm was still around me and he leaned down to talk softly into my ear. "Come on, let's get you out of here."

I let him lead me out, not bothering to say goodbye. I was a little afraid that if I opened my mouth at all I would burst out in sobs. Or I'd start shrieking and cursing like some kind of crazed psycho.

There was a very good likelihood that I'd crush Tina like a bug.

Instead I let him guide me through the crowd, which

was no longer paying attention to me. I was back to being invisible and for the first time in my life, I was totally okay with that.

It wasn't until we were outside and nearing the street that he spoke. "You okay?"

I nodded. "I guess."

His voice was so close and his arm was still wrapped around me. I should have minded, but I didn't. He was comforting. Whether he knew who I was or not, he was the closest thing I had to a real friend at this party.

I could still hear Melody's shocked laughter, mixed in with everyone else's as I'd been humiliated in her kitchen.

I stopped walking so abruptly, Drew kept going and nearly knocked me over with his arm. He stopped and looked down at me.

"No," I said. "Actually, I'm not all right." Anger made my stomach queasy and my hands clenched into fists. "I'm cold and I'm wet." I shook off his arm so I could spin around and storm back into the house. "I am so going to kick some ass."

"Whoa, whoa." He grabbed my shoulders and brought me to a halt before I could go more than a few steps. He leaned down so his mouth was close to my ear, keeping his voice low as some latecomers to the party walked past us, calling out a hello to Drew.

"You can confront Tina at school on Monday. If you still want to kick her ass, I'll help hold the others back so you can have at her. All right?"

I heard the teasing note in his voice and had to fight a smile at the image of him with his arms out, holding back the rest of the school so I could give Tina the ass kicking she deserved.

"Trust me," he continued softly. "You need to calm

down first. Get your head on straight. Don't give her or that crowd the satisfaction of any more drama."

Those last words finally did the trick. I stopped trying to resist him, letting him spin me back around so we were heading away from the house. "Where are we going?"

His arm rested lightly on my shoulders as he guided me down the street to the right. "My car. I'll take you home."

He helped me into the passenger's side of his car as if I was sick or elderly. Or maybe he was just worried that I'd try to run back to the house and start throwing punches.

The thought made me laugh.

He was buckling his seat belt and glanced over with a hesitant smile. "Feeling better?"

I shrugged. "Just plotting my revenge."

His smile widened and I lost the ability to breathe as one of his dimples appeared. Man, this kid had the best smile ever. It could be his superpower. No villain could resist the power of the dimple.

"How evil are we talking?" he asked. "Are we talking *Carrie* levels of retribution?"

I pretended to mull it over. "More like *Kill Bill*."

He tossed his head back with a laugh and I found myself grinning at him despite everything. He had a great laugh. And that smile... have I mentioned how sexy that smile was?

Criminally hot.

He turned to face me again and he wielded that sexy smile like a weapon. I swear I could feel it all the way in my gut.

"Remind me not to get on your bad side," he said.

Too late. I managed to return his smile. Because in this moment, forgetting who I was paled in comparison to what his friends just did.

"I can't believe you're friends with those people," I said without thinking. Because who was I to know anything about him or his friendships.

He didn't seem to mind. He just shrugged. "Yeah, well. I'm friendly with them. I wouldn't exactly call them friends."

I snuck a glance at him. Then who were his friends? Because according to Trent and Margo, my sources back at Atwater, he wasn't spending time with his old friends either. Or maybe he'd just been friendly with them too.

Unbelievably I felt a pang of pity for Mr. Popular. But really, for someone so popular he didn't seem to have friends. I was definitely not popular but at least I had Trent, Margo, and the guys.

He pulled the car out of the parking spot and it was only then that I realized he didn't know where I lived. Or, he didn't know where Veronica lived, at least. I cleared my throat. "Um, if you take a right up here—"

"I know where you live, Ronnie." His voice was low and gentle but I jerked back and sucked in air like he'd just slapped me across the face.

Ronnie. He'd called me Ronnie.

Oh crap, he remembered me. But even as I thought it, I felt a wave of relief. And complete and utter embarrassment. I was being buffeted by a tsunami of conflicting emotions and it was confusing the hell out of me.

Drew, meanwhile, looked irritatingly calm, cool, and collected. He even gave me a quick smile. "I played pin the tail on the donkey at your backyard birthday parties enough times that I'm pretty sure I could find it blindfolded."

Awesome. Drew was so confident and relaxed he was making corny jokes while I sat there trying not to hyperventilate. But then, he wasn't the one who'd pretended to be someone he wasn't.

No. I shook my head slightly. I wasn't pretending to be someone else, I was being a more confident, well-rounded me. The best version of me. I was faking it until I made it.

Somehow all the self-help jargon didn't make a dent in how ridiculous I felt. In fact, right now they weren't making much sense to my panicked, frazzled brain. Best version of me... what did that even mean? What version of me was I before? And fake it until I made *what*, exactly?

I thought back to the party tonight and had to fight a wave of hysterical laughter. Well, I guess I'd made it. I'd certainly become visible. A hot guy had asked me out—only to make his girlfriend jealous, but hey, minor detail. And the popular girls loved me—until they threw their beer on me.

In my attempt to keep from laughing, I let out a snort-laugh that was so utterly old Ronnie, it made me laugh for real. I caught a glimpse of Drew giving me an uncertain smile. "Are you all right?"

"Never better," I said as my laughter faded.

There was an awkward silence. Maybe he was waiting for me to explain the whole Ronnie-Veronica thing, or maybe he was trying to figure out what question to ask first. Either way, I didn't want to hear it. "Thanks for the ride," I said quickly, hoping to fill the silence and divert the conversation. "And thanks for, uh... you know."

"Pretending I was your date?" he asked.

"Yeah that."

I couldn't bring myself to look at his face so I watched his hands grip the steering wheel and then relax. Grip and relax. It looked like a nervous habit. Why would he be nervous? Maybe because he's driving home the weirdo who pretended she didn't know who he was. Or maybe because he'd just announced we were dating to half the junior class.

That triggered a memory—many memories, actually—of all the girls at Briarwood who'd mentioned how Drew doesn't date. Ever. Apparently he'd gone to great lengths to make that known. And now tonight, thanks to me, that whole player rep was blown to pieces.

Oops.

I shifted in my seat and bit my lip as I tried to come up with the right words. It was a weird thing to apologize for, but then, who was I to judge? I knew what it was to have a reputation—wanted or otherwise—and clearly this was one he wanted, and I'd destroyed that.

"Sorry," I said, the word coming out stilted and awkward.

"For what?" He sounded genuinely confused.

"For, uh... I'm sorry that people think you date now," I said. I cast a quick glance and saw him giving me a little smile. One that clearly said "I like you but you're crazy."

"It's cool," he said. "It wasn't like I set out to have a reputation for not dating," he said. "It just kind of happened."

I nibbled on my lip as I took in his profile—his way too gorgeous for life profile. "Because you don't date," I clarified.

He nodded. "Exactly."

I shouldn't ask. I shouldn't bring up Atwater. I should continue to act like we're strangers. I should— "But you used to."

Damn my stupid mouth and its stupid lack of a filter. Curiosity had gotten the best of me. It was a question that had been nagging at me for a while now, ever since I'd first heard the rumors about the great, undateable Drew Remi.

He shot me a look before returning his attention to the road, then he shifted in his seat, visibly uncomfortable.

Way to go, Ronnie. The guy comes to your rescue like some knight in shining armor and in return you make him feel bad. Nicely done.

"Never mind," I said.

At the same exact time, he said, "I guess you mean April."

The silence was back. I could hear my own heartbeat in the awkwardness. Well, wasn't this pleasant? I fought for a topic that would put us back on even ground. Half turning in my seat, I offered, "You want to hear my diabolical plans for Alex?"

It had the desired effect. Drew smiled that sexy smile again, glancing over at me. "Alex? I thought you were going to exact your revenge on Tina for, uh..." His eyes dropped down to my wet top, which I now realized was clinging to my body like second skin.

My cheeks may have caught on fire I was so freakin' embarrassed. I glanced over and noticed that his face was unusually flushed too.

Well, at least I wasn't the only uncomfortable one. Crossing my arms over my body in a futile attempt to hide myself, I explained my reasoning. "Don't worry, I fully intend to take Tina down, but right now Alex is first on the vengeance hit list."

My light tone seemed to help the tension levels in the car fall back to status quo, which was awkward but not humiliating.

"And why's that?" His voice turned hard as he cast me a far more serious look. "Did he do something? Ronnie, I swear, if he came on too strong or—"

"No!" I said quickly. I knew where he was going with

this and needed to cut off his suspicions before they got out of control. "Nothing like that."

At his questioning silence, I continued. "He didn't take me to dinner."

I watched Drew blink a couple of times. He pulled up in front of my house before turning to stare at me. "Excuse me?"

I sighed and then explained the whole embarrassing night because, honestly, at this point I wasn't sure I could be any more humiliated in front of Drew Remi. Besides, now he knew I was Ronnie, so why not be honest?

Now it was impossible to pretend I was "the best version of me." This guy had known me since birth, practically. He knew me just like I knew him. Sure, we might not have been the best of friends but we had a shared history.

I was humiliated by the night in general and about being caught pretending not to know who he was, but it was a relief. Being around him felt much easier now that I didn't have to worry about pretending to be someone I'm not or not knowing things about him, like that he'd cried while watching *An American Tail* that one time in Mrs. Dumfry's class.

So as we sat there in the darkness of his car, I told him about how Alex had asked me, the weird comment my teammate had made, the way Alex had eaten already and assumed that I had too. I told him how it had all unraveled in the kitchen right up until he'd stepped in.

I ended with a sad sigh as I let my head drop back against the seat. "Thank God this night is over."

I rolled my head to the side to see that he was giving me a smile—a small one that was comforting and oddly sweet. I had no idea Drew Remi could do sweet. It seemed his smiles knew no bounds.

"So what I'm hearing is, you're hungry."

I stared at him, surprised by his teasing, comfortable tone as much as the glimmer of humor in his eyes.

Ugh, could he get any hotter? It just wasn't fair. He didn't even seem to try. He was just naturally charming and sweet and sexy and—gah! I was staring. I shook my head quickly and reached for the door. "Starving. And desperately in need of a change."

His hand on mine made me freeze and heat up all at the same time. My brain felt like scrambled eggs at the light touch. I turned back to see him giving me that lopsided grin that made my belly do backflips. "I don't know about you, but it's Saturday night and I really don't want the night to end at eight o'clock or with either of us starving to death."

I stared at him, my mind a blank. All of my attention was focused on his hand on mine. What was he saying? I felt too stupid to understand anything more complicated than one syllable action verbs.

"Let's eat," he said. "Together." When I was still quiet he looked a little less certain but still just as cute. "Unless you don't want to, in which case—"

"I do." I blurted it out and then realized just how much it sounded like I was exchanging vows. "I mean, I do want to eat. With you."

Ugh, I was never speaking again. After tonight I was swearing off the English language. Maybe I'd learn sign language or something.

"Great." He sat back in his seat and released my hand. I was now able to breathe. And move.

I pointed at my house. "I'll just, uh... I'll be right back."

I tried not to run into my house because I was trying to play it cool. No, I wasn't trying to *fake it till I make it*. Not with Drew, at least. No amount of faking it would fool someone who's known me my whole life. But I was attempting to be cool.

Cool for Ronnie, which was really not all that cool. But it did involve not running and squealing around the new hot friend.

I came to a screeching halt when I hit my bedroom. Was that what Drew was? My friend?

I shrugged out of my shirt and grabbed a change of clothes to slip into after a super quick shower. Thankfully it was date night for my parents, otherwise how the hell would I explain the fact that I smelled like a brewery?

I pulled my hair back in a loose ponytail after I washed up and threw on a clean shirt. Another T-shirt but this one didn't cling and I felt far more comfortable. I also swapped out the skirt for a pair of faded, comfy jeans. After all, there was no impressing Drew. No amount of fancy clothes or primping would change the fact that he knew me—the class tomboy, and the gangly, non-girlie, not-popular nobody.

As I headed out feeling comfortable for once, I didn't care about any of that. All I cared about was revelling in the fact that I wasn't suffocating in clothes. And that very soon I would be eating.

I was seriously starving.

SIX

Drew

I WATCHED Veronica eat her pizza with unabashed abandon. It was a beautiful sight, really. She was no less beautiful now that I knew she was Ronnie, but she looked different. And it wasn't just the more relaxed clothing or the fact that her hair was pulled back in a low ponytail.

It was hard to explain but knowing who she was—knowing she was the same Ronnie who'd helped me walk home when I'd skinned my knees on the way home from the park in third grade, the girl whose mom always brought soccer-themed cakes to the in-school birthday parties—it made my view of her shift like a kaleidoscope.

Watching her take another bite of pepperoni pizza I felt it click into place. She came into focus.

"Are you just going to sit there and stare at me while I eat?" she asked. Her gaze never left the slice of pizza in her hands as if she was afraid someone was going to come along and snatch it from her.

I grinned. Now that sounded like the Ronnie I remembered. Snarky and sarcastic and not even a tiny bit giggly.

Her gaze shot up to meet mine and my smile faltered. This was Ronnie, all right. And this was also Veronica. Man, how had I never noticed how pretty she was before? Had she always been this hot?

She was waiting for me to respond, obviously, so I forced a smirk. This was Ronnie, after all. "Sorry, I've just never seen a girl inhale an entire pizza before. You should think about entering an eating competition."

For a half second I thought she'd balk. Most girls would not love to have their eating habits pointed out and mocked.

But most girls were not Ronnie.

She smiled at me as she chewed and the smile made her dark eyes brighten and her face light up. "Maybe I should," she said. "It sounds like a pretty awesome gig."

We sat there smiling at each other in silence for way too long. I'd forgotten what we were talking about, to be honest. I was too busy marveling at this change in Ronnie... or in the new version of Veronica.

I was confused, obviously. But it wasn't every day the girl you've been crushing on ends up being the tomboy you've known since birth.

I had so many questions for her but I had no idea how to start. I guess I was a little afraid of hearing the answers, too. It really all came down to one question. Why hadn't she told me she was Ronnie?

Maybe because she thought you would have recognized her. Maybe she wanted nothing to do with her elementary school friend. Or maybe—

"You're doing it again," she pointed out.

I was staring. Again. Creepily, no doubt. I shook my

head with a laugh. "Sorry, I'm just still getting used to this." I glanced up and met her gaze. "You look different."

She let out a little snort of amusement that was pure Ronnie. "I should hope so."

He blinked at her. What did that mean?

She set down her slice and waved vaguely in the direction of her face and hair. "Do you have any idea how much time and energy it takes to look like this?" She curled her lip up disgust. "Such a waste."

I laughed. I couldn't help it. She was just so Ronnie. How had I not seen it before? Maybe I'd been blinded by her beauty...literally. "I guess I don't know how long it takes, but I will say that you look amazing."

Was it possible? Was Ronnie Smith blushing? Something about that blush made my chest feel too tight, and breathing became difficult. This was a whole new side of Ronnie.

The girl was like an endless riddle. I'd always known her as the class tomboy—if asked before this week I would have said she was average looking, into soccer, and kept to herself at school.

But now? Now I realized I didn't really know Ronnie. Or Veronica, for that matter. I would never have guessed that Veronica played soccer if I hadn't seen it with my own eyes. And up until tonight I would have said she was a girlie girl who was into clothes and shopping, and had loads of girl friends.

That thought made me think of what had happened earlier in the night and I felt my stomach churn on her behalf. I thought of Alex's face as he reveled in the limelight. And what an ass. I'd never thought of him as a great friend, just a teammate, but we'd been friendly.

Until tonight.

I clenched my hands so hard some soda sloshed over the side of my paper cup. At Veronica's questioning look, I forced myself to relax. "So, if you hate doing *this*..." I copied her vague waving gesture. "Why do it?"

It was the wrong question to ask. I could tell that instantly in the way her nostrils flared and she took a deep breath as if praying for patience. "You wouldn't understand."

She wasn't particularly mean in the way she said it but the words were enough. It made me stiffen. "What's that supposed to mean?"

She shrugged and went back to eating. "It means you wouldn't understand."

I don't know why this bothered me so much but I didn't like the way she was writing me off. Like she knew everything about me and had already decided what I would and would not understand. "Because I'm not a girl?"

She shrugged again. "That and other reasons."

"Like what?"

She shot me a quick look of annoyance before setting down her pizza with a sigh. "You wouldn't get it because you've always been popular."

Oh.

She gave me a smug smile before taking a sip of her water.

For some reason that smug smile brought back that feeling of annoyance. What did Veronica know about me and my popularity?

Everything, a little voice reminded me. *She's known you forever.*

Yes, but she *didn't* know everything. She saw what everyone saw—the guy who had it all. And for a long time I'd seen myself that way. Up until everything fell apart.

First my parents' marriage, then my friendships as I'd been forced to go to California, then my relationship with April when she'd broken up with me.... The list went on and on. After a lifetime of being blessed, this past year it seemed like nothing was going right.

The only thing that hadn't failed me was baseball. Every school had a team and unless my arm gave out on me or I got in an accident or something, I would excel at it.

It was the one thing I could count on.

She'd gone back to eating but I wasn't through. Tonight, the only thing I hated more than Alex, Tina, and that crowd was the way Veronica was writing me off.

"Try me." I crossed my arms over my chest and leveled her with a glare that would have made most girls? people? back down.

Not Veronica.

She widened her eyes in surprise but then grinned as she set down her glass and folded her arms just like I'd done. "Okay, hotshot. When's the last time you were invisible?"

Bam. Her words punched me in the gut. No, not her words so much as the look in her eyes. There was an age-old hurt there and I knew in that moment that I was to blame.

Well, maybe not just me, but I was a part of whatever pain she'd experienced. I wanted to apologize but didn't know how. Hell, I didn't even know what I'd be apologizing for. "You've never been invisible," I said.

She gave another snort but this time it was less amused and far more mocking. "Oh really?" she said. "Then why didn't you recognize me when I literally ran right into you at Briarwood?"

I flinched. Good question. I'd been asking myself the same thing.

I still didn't have an answer. My silence seemed to be all the answer she needed because she continued on as if I'd just made her point. "You see? You didn't recognize me because you didn't remember me. I was just some girl you went to school with. You didn't know me. Once popularity became a thing, I was forgotten."

"You have friends," I said. I could picture Ronnie at Atwater walking down the hall with a group of guys, joking and laughing.

"Of course I have friends," she snapped. "I'm not a leper."

I shrugged. "So how are you invisible then? You have *friends*." I said it with too much emphasis, probably giving away some of my own anger.

As I spoke I kept thinking about my friends—my *former* friends. Sure I'd been popular, but did I ever have any true friends?

"I have great friends. Excellent friends. I'm not looking for any more good friends," she said, her words tumbling out quickly. "But you don't know what it's like to be surrounded by people who've known you forever but who don't *know* you."

I stared at her. I'm pretty sure my horror was written plainly on my face. She'd lost me after her little tirade about her awesome, wonderful friends. "Do you hear yourself? You have friends. Good friends. What more do you need?"

She shook her head so quickly her ponytail whipped back and forth. "But that doesn't change the fact that I've been invisible my whole life." She stopped suddenly, and her eyes filled with pain as she rolled her eyes. "Until tonight, at least." She dropped her head into her hands with a moan and I forgot my irritation. It melted away instantly at the sight of her looking so miserable.

I'd been so into our conversation I'd almost forgotten how this all began. Without thinking I reached over and placed one hand on her arm in support. She stiffened at my touch but didn't pull away.

"Those guys back there are jackholes," I said, using the stupid term my sister and I had made up years ago to avoid cursing at home. "They don't deserve to be friends with you."

After a brief hesitation, she peeked up and I felt a rush of relief to see that she was smiling slightly. "They are *jackholes*, aren't they?"

I laughed as she repeated my lame insult. "Total jackholes."

She dropped her hands and sat up straight again. "I can't believe I actually thought that they liked me."

"They probably do like you," I felt compelled to say. I don't know why I was sticking up for that crowd but I needed to see her smile again. "What happened tonight wasn't about you. It was about them."

She arched one eyebrow. "That sounds like something my grandma would tell me to make me feel better."

I grinned. "Well, your grandma would be right."

She rolled her eyes and I could tell she didn't believe me. Leaning forward, I took one of her hands in mine. I'd opened my mouth to speak but temporarily forgot what I was going to say at the feel of her warm skin. Electricity seemed to leap from her hand to mine.

She leaned forward a bit, giving me an expectant look and I pushed away the stupid attraction to focus on Ronnie, my once-upon-a-time friend. "I'm not being nice when I say that it's not about you," I said. "The more you hang out with those people, the more you'll notice that most popular people are popular because they're always thinking about themselves. They are self-absorbed and other people buy into that."

"Wow."

For half a second I thought maybe she was blown away by my insight. But then a teasing smile hovered over her lips. "Jaded much?"

I laughed. Yeah, I guess I was pretty jaded. I'd been hanging with a popular crowd for as long as Ronnie had been feeling invisible. I tilted my head from one side to the other as though deliberating her words. "Maybe I'm a *little* cynical these days."

When I met her gaze again, I was surprised to see her studying me. "What happened?"

"What do you mean?" Playing dumb seemed like a good idea.

She didn't fall for it, obviously. "What happened to make you so cynical about your friends?"

The truth came blurting out before I could stop it. "I guess I just discovered that they weren't really my friends."

I'm not sure what I was expecting. Maybe more questions or some teasing mockery at my earnestness. But she just turned her hand in mine so it was palm up and squeezed. "I'm sorry."

I shrugged. "It's fine."

It wasn't fine. But at that particular moment, with her hand in mine and no one else around, life seemed pretty perfect.

Her sad sigh had my gaze focusing on her face again—this face that was both my old friend Ronnie and my new crush Veronica. I was starting to get used to this new version of them both.

And I liked it. I liked *her*.

Oh hell. I felt a tugging in my chest that let me know

just how much of an understatement that was. I liked her a lot. Like, more than I liked old friend Ronnie and much more than I'd crushed on new hottie Veronica.

This feeling was new and intense, and I was in so much trouble.

She bit her lip and I tried not to focus on her lips. This was Ronnie. A friend... maybe. Hopefully. Then she tilted her head to the side and gave me a mischievous grin that set my heartrate soaring.

"Want to talk about it?" she asked, her voice impossibly sweet.

I met her smile because it was impossible not to. I was having the best time I'd had in a long time. I had no desire to think about April or Lee so I shook my head. "Not really."

"But how will I know who I should add to my vengeance list if you don't name names?"

I blinked at her. I'd been so lost in these crazy new emotions it took me a minute to register what she'd said. Her smile grew along with her teasing tone as she pointed to herself. "I'm kicking ass and taking names over here, Drew. You might want to get in on this."

I laughed, all thoughts of April and the others evaporating along with the terrifying paralysis that came with realizing I had a major thing for Ronnie Smith. Or Veronica Smith, whatever.

"I'm serious," she said, her eyes comically wide. "Especially if some girl did something to make you this jaded. Because honestly, you might not be able to get away with a bitch slap but I totally can." She flexed her arms like Hulk Hogan. "Bring it."

My face hurt from smiling. Had it really been that long since I'd genuinely laughed with a friend that my face muscles had gone weak? Apparently so.

She didn't let up, prodding and teasing until I spilled the truth. By that point, the wave of hurt was gone, thanks to my new good mood so I told her the embarrassing truth about how my ex had dumped me for my friend weeks after I'd left.

Her teasing stopped as soon as I told her. Her pretty eyes grew soft and sad, but not filled with pity, thankfully. I don't think I could have handled pity, not from her.

"April did that?" she asked.

I nodded. I could have just let it go but my mouth seemed to have other plans. "The worst part about that breakup wasn't really the breakup." I rolled my eyes. "I mean, yeah it sucked, but I wasn't naïve enough to think a high school relationship like ours would work long distance for long."

"Like yours?" she repeated.

I gave her a rundown of what our relationship was like —mainly, how it had been centered around other people. Not just us. We'd hooked up for the first time at a party and most of our "dates" took place at parties or with a group of friends. We were part of the same group, had the same friends. It seemed to make sense that our relationship involved them.

Veronica wrinkled her nose at me. "No offense, but that sounds weird. I mean, my only experience with relationships is watching my best friend, Trent, and his girlfriend from the sidelines but I'd think it was weird if they didn't take some solo time."

I nodded. I remembered Trent and Margo, but it was news to me that they were together. She shook her head as if annoyed with the distraction. "Sorry, you were saying that it wasn't just the breakup that sucked."

"it was the timing of it all," I said. "My parents had just

split. My sister and I were caught up in a custody battle. It was just... crappy timing."

That was putting it mildly.

"Crappy timing," she repeated under her breath. "That's an understatement. I mean, going through family issues must've been bad enough but to lose your friends and your girlfriend at the same time..."

She didn't finish and she didn't need to. It sucked.

I cleared my throat. "Yeah, well...Tonight's not about me and my sucky year, it's about you and your craptastic night."

She held up her bottle of water to cheers my soda. "Here's to all the jackholes. May we never have to deal with them again."

I let out a huff of laughter. "That's easier said than done." I arched one brow as I stated the obvious. "My jackholes are back at Atwater."

"And I have to see mine on Monday morning," she finished glumly.

I hated to see her smile falter. "I've got your back. Besides, you and that scene will be old news by Monday morning. My guess is a ton of drama went down after we left."

She wrinkled her nose. "Seriously? That sounds... exhausting."

I nodded. "Trust me, it is."

"Was it like that with your friends back at Atwater?"

I nodded again. "Oh yeah. Same exact situation, except there I never had to go through the hell of being the new kid." I gave her a pointed look. She knew exactly what it meant to be the new person in that kind of crowd.

She shook her head with a wince. "It's like dealing with a pack of hyenas or something."

I laughed as I agreed. "There are a lot of similarities to the animal kingdom. It's all about dominance."

She met my gaze, apparently trying to figure out if I was joking. I wasn't, not really. She shook her head again. "Like I said... exhausting."

I had to agree. Even back at Atwater, it had been hard to keep up with all the drama. "That's why I keep my distance," I said. "After April, I just couldn't deal with the games anymore. She was always looking to stir up drama or mess with my head."

She raised her brows in surprise. "That's why you don't date?"

I lifted one shoulder in a half shrug. "That's part of it. I need to stay focused this year if I want to get a baseball scholarship." I hesitated before continuing. "But, yeah, part of it's because I'm tired of the drama." I grinned as I echoed her words. "I guess I'm just exhausted."

"Understandably."

I found myself watching her, fascinated by the way her eyes seemed to change color with her emotions. I felt that tug again, that incessant feeling that seemed to be pulling me toward her.

I wanted to kiss her.

More than anything in the world, at that moment I wanted to kiss her.

Which was totally illogical since I had literally just explained why I didn't date anymore. But Veronica was different. She wasn't any other girl I knew. Of course, that made her that much more dangerous. She was an unknown entity. Who knew how she would affect my life? I already knew that she'd messed with my concentration and that was before... this. The new, overwhelming sensation of having a crush on someone I actually liked as a person. As a friend, even. Maybe. Hopefully.

I felt something I hadn't felt in ages. Nerves. I cleared my throat again as if that would help. "So, are we..." Oh man, I wasn't really going to say it, was I?

She gave me an expectant look. "Are we what?"

"Friends," I finished. "Are we friends now?" I tried to add a joking tone, make it a teasing question and not let on just how much her answer meant.

She looked at me like I was nuts. "Of course."

I grinned. Of course. I liked that. I could settle for friends.

Her smile widened and she raised her bottle again. "To friends," she said. "And to no more games."

Hell yeah, I could cheers to that. "To no more games."

SEVEN

Veronica

FRIENDS. Drew Remi wanted to be friends. A full twenty-four hours later and I still couldn't quite wrap my head around this new turn of events.

I sat in Trent's basement with him and Margo. They'd insisted that I come over to hang out on Sunday night before school began. Some of the guys were coming over too—Sunday nights at Trent's was a longstanding tradition, just like videogames after school was tradition. But Sunday nights involved *Doctor Who* marathons or binge-watching the Marvel movies. They were a night to camp out in front of his family's old TV and forget the Sunday blues.

My Sunday blues should have been through-the-roof bad. I mean, tomorrow morning I was going to have to face the people who'd laughed at me, like Melody and her friends. Not to mention Alex and Tina, the stars of last night's melodrama.

Maybe Drew was right. Maybe it wouldn't be so bad.

Maybe they really had forgotten and I was the only one who was obsessing over it.

To be fair, I was only obsessing over the beer-in-face incident when I wasn't obsessing over my conversation with Drew Remi.

In the grand scope of things, it was hard to say which was more surreal—living the kind of horrifying high school party moment I thought only took place in cheesy teen movies or having a one-on-one bonding night with Drew Remi.

Drew Remi. He was not just another former classmate, he was *the* former classmate. He was the kid who'd been too cool for the rest of us. He'd been the one who led the high school baseball team to championships when he was a freshman.

This was the alpha male who every guy wanted to be and every girl secretly wanted to date. No one could admit it, of course, because every girl was at least a little bit afraid of April Ramsey.

Including me.

Oh, I wasn't *scared*-scared. I knew I could take her in a fight, just like I could take Tina. But she was intimidating in her own way. She was socially powerful, if not physically terrifying.

Kind of like Tina.

Margo sank down onto the seat next to me. "Want to talk about it?"

I cringed, not because Margo had bad breath or something but because she was such a girl. And I don't mean that in a mean way, I mean it in an "I'm a weirdo" way, because I wished it came easily to me, opening up like that. To see a friend hanging out and be like "hey, want to talk?"

No. I'd spent too much time with Trent and the other

guys. Even my former teammates and I didn't do that kind of thing. We razzed each other, we had inside jokes and sat silently and played video games beside one another for hours on end. But have deep, meaningful one-on-one talks?

I don't think so.

Not until Margo came into my life. And now, apparently, Drew Remi. Because whether I could fully wrap my head around it or not, he and I had talked. Like seriously talked. Like, he'd opened up to me about past relationships kind of talked.

My mind was still blown.

And Margo was still watching me. If there was anyone who could make sense of any of this, it was her. She might not be crazy popular like Drew or insanely trying to reinvent herself like me, but she definitely had more emotional intelligence than I did.

Heck, she had more emotional intelligence than the rest of us in this room combined.

As if sensing my weakness, she grabbed me by the hand and tugged, leading me upstairs to Trent's room.

It was weird being in this room with Margo. It was a room from my past and when I looked around all I saw was the Lego's Millennium Falcon that I'd helped him build and the poster for *Lord of the Rings*, which always reminds me of that weekend we thought it would be fun to watch the extended cuts for all the movies.

Twenty-something hours of non-stop hobbits wasn't so much *fun* as it was a serious undertaking, but we'd discovered an odd sense of pride by the end, like we'd accomplished something huge.

All of that I was used to. But being here with Margo I saw it through her point of view. I noticed the framed picture of the two of them in a place of prominence on his nightstand. I noticed the old movie tickets that were probably from their first date or something—Trent was alarmingly romantic about that kind of stuff. And then my gaze fell on his bed, which I realized was where they probably kissed and made out and stuff.

I looked away quickly. *Ew.*

I mean, making out isn't gross and part of my whole "new Veronica" experiment was so I could have my first kiss, finally, and maybe even have a boyfriend. But still, thinking of Trent like that made me uncomfortable and being here with Margo made it impossible to ignore.

We were growing up. We were changing. Trent was in love and in an actual relationship. And me? Well, apparently I was friends with Drew Remi.

And I wasn't sure that was what I wanted. Let me rephrase—I wasn't sure that was *all* I wanted. Obviously I found Drew attractive. Every girl with functioning eyes found Drew attractive. But I'd never thought of him like that—not until last night.

So yeah. Trent was in a real relationship and I was having feelings for Drew Remi.

We were officially in new territory here, folks. Life was changing. I know that's what I'd wanted, but right now it all seemed to be happening too fast.

Margo, apparently not sharing my ick factor over the unmade bed, sat down on its edge and patted the spot next to her.

I sat beside her with a sigh. I was officially defeated. My head and my heart were in turmoil and I needed girl guidance in a bad way.

"Okay, spill," she said. When I didn't start immediately, she persisted. "What happened at the party? You've been weirdly tight-lipped."

I wanted to tell her, I really did. But talking about this stuff was hard. It meant reliving that awful moment.

Now it was her turn to sigh as she shifted so she was fully facing me, pulling her legs up beneath her. "Ronnie, after all the time I spent helping you get ready, you owe me this."

She was teasing, but it worked. No one deserved to hear the end result of all that work more than Margo. I shifted so I was facing her too and told her everything...about the party. I wasn't ready to dive into Drew territory yet. I didn't want to tell her, or anyone, for that matter, all that he'd told me about April and his parents and I wasn't sure how to talk about our bonding over pizza without mentioning that stuff.

So I focused on the party, actually getting into it as I realized I had a rapt audience in Margo. She stared wide-eyed as I told her about the confrontation, and then her eyes grew impossibly wide when I told her about the beer being thrown in my face. She even gasped in outrage, which was incredibly satisfying as a storyteller.

"She didn't!" Margo said.

I nodded. "She did."

Margo leaned forward. "Then what happened?"

I hesitated for half a second before the words tumbled out and I filled her in on Drew's rescue.

She seemed even more stunned by that than by the Tina showdown. A silence followed once I stopped talking and Margo was not only wide-eyed, but her mouth was partially open. I now knew what the term *dumbstruck* meant.

Finally, she blinked. "Oh my God," she said, her voice syrupy sweet. "That is so romantic."

I frowned at her. What? No. Clearly she'd misunderstood. "Margo, he wasn't really my date. He just said that to—"

"To save you," Margo cut in. "He was your knight in shining armor." She clutched her hands to her chest. "That is so sweet."

Knight in shining *what?* No. Just no.

Hells no.

I wasn't a romantic and I absolutely didn't need a knight, in shining armor or any other type of armor. Yes, he'd come to my rescue... in a sense. But he was just being nice. And there sure as hell wasn't anything romantic about it.

But try telling Margo that. If we were in a cartoon, little hearts would be swirling in those big blue eyes of hers. One would think she was the damsel in distress who'd been rescued from a tower, not me.

Not that I *was* a damsel in distress.

Oh crap. Now she had me thinking in those stupid, misogynistic fairytale metaphors. That more than anything had me crossing my arms and scowling at her. "It's not like that," I said. I had a vivid memory of the way our talk had ended. Friends. We were friends.

"He was just helping me out," I said. "As a friend."

The words stuck in my throat. It felt even weirder to say it aloud. Friends. Me and Drew, best buds.

Something in me refused to buy it. It was like trying to convince myself that I liked brussels sprouts.

Okay, so it wasn't exactly like that. Drew and brussels sprouts had zero in common. One was hot, sexy, charming, and shockingly nice. The other smelled as bad as it tasted.

Maybe that wasn't the best comparison, but the point was—no matter how much I tried to sell myself on the idea, the thought of me and Drew being friends didn't sit right.

Why?

Because I liked him.

I groaned softly as the truth of it hit me and there was no denying it any longer.

I had a crush on Drew Remi.

Why, God, why? I'd resisted his allure for years. Years! I'd prided myself on being the only girl at Atwater who didn't harbor a crush on the untouchable baseball star. So why now?

Maybe because he was no longer untouchable. I had a vision of Drew with those warm brown eyes and that ridiculously adorable grin. Of the sad tinge to his gaze as he'd opened up about his ex and his family.

He'd seemed so real. So normal, albeit stupidly attractive.

"What's wrong?" Margo asked, most likely because my groan had sounded more like a wail.

I turned my pathetic gaze to her and told her the truth. "I think I like Drew Remi."

Again with the wailing. Margo looked sweetly sympathetic for about half a second. Then she burst out laughing.

"Hey! This isn't funny." But watching Margo-the-Kindhearted laugh at me made me laugh too before I reached for a pillow to smack her.

"Ow!" She took the pillow from me, still laughing but not so hard now. "I'm sorry, it's just... of course you do."

I opened my mouth to protest and explain just how long I'd resisted his charms, but she was too quick. "Obviously you have a crush. First of all, he's totally crush-worthy. If you didn't have at least a little bit of a crush, you wouldn't have a pulse."

I tilted my head to one said as I considered that. "Fair point."

"And second," she continued. "This totally crush-worthy hottie came to your rescue. Whether you believe in Prince Charming or not, there's no denying that his heroic rescue in the face of public humiliation was *hot*."

I stared at her for a moment. She seemed so sure of herself, and oddly enough her reasoning made me feel better. Maybe this weird, needy longing feeling I had in my chest every time I thought of Drew was really just a side effect of last night's drama. It would probably fade away, just like my humiliation and anger.

Though none of those emotions showed any signs of fading anytime soon. Just the thought of Tina's smug face and Melody's laughter had my hands curling into fists on my lap.

"Okay, where did you just go?" Margo said, cutting into my anger. "One second you were normal Ronnie and then bam—" She thwacked the pillow. "Incredible Hulk Ronnie came out of hiding."

I let out a surprised laugh at the image of me turning into the Incredible Hulk and made a concerted effort to relax my fists. "Sorry, I'm still furious every time I think about those girls."

I managed to make *those girls* sound like a curse word and Margo let out a short laugh. "Yeah, they sound horrible."

I nodded. They were horrible. Except that... they weren't. Or they hadn't been. I'd started to think that Melody was my friend. I'd started to get to know a few of the girls from the team, but Melody was the one I sat with every day, the one who'd sought me out in the hall. "I thought we were friends." My voice was so gloomy, I cleared my throat and shook my head. "That sounds pathetic, but I guess it's true." I shrugged helplessly. "I thought for the first time that I had a real girl friend. Not teammates who I'm friendly with because we have soccer in common, but an honest to God girl friend."

Margo was quiet for a second and I thought maybe I'd wowed her with my insights. But then I turned to face her and saw the most unexpected sight I could ever have imagined.

Margo looked pissed. "What am I, exactly?"

Oh. Um...oops. "Margo, I didn't mean—"

Margo held up air quotes as she repeated my words and I felt so guilty I couldn't even mock her for it. "For the first time I had a girl friend.... An honest-to-God girl friend..." She dropped the air quotes. "What am *I*, exactly?

I winced and gave her my most apologetic, sheepish grin. It didn't work. She was staring at me, waiting for an answer.

"Um, you're Trent's girlfriend?" And yes, it came out as a question like I was on *Jeopardy* or something.

She scoffed and folded her arms in front of her chest. "So, what, that's all I am?"

I tried to make this right. "You're also my kind, angelic fairy godmother who singlehandedly transformed me from hopeless tomboy to this." I gestured to my sweatpants and oversized T-shirt and wagged my eyebrows. "This hotness."

She pinched her lips together, clearly fighting not to laugh.

In my defense, I was about to curl up on an old, smelly couch with a group of loud, smelly boys and watch some truly wonderful and geeky sci-fi while I avoided the emotional turmoil that was my life. I'd assumed mission "new and improved Veronica" was temporarily on hold for the evening.

"You do look hot," Margo said with a straight face.

We both burst out laughing at the ridiculously false statement. But then she straightened and it was her turn to swat me with the pillow. "For the record, though, I consider you a friend. And not just because you're Trent's best friend, either."

I could feel my cheeks getting hot at her honesty. I also felt a surge of gratitude that this kind, fashionable girl had come into my life. To show her just how grateful I was, I did something totally un-Ronnie-like and leaned forward to give her a hug.

Unlike me, Margo was a hugger so I knew she'd appreciate it. She also knew that I didn't do touchy feely hugs so she'd know what I was trying to say.

Still, I said it anyway. "Thanks for being my friend."

EIGHT

Drew

IT WAS WEDNESDAY, which meant the last playoff game was tonight. There was nothing in this world more important than this game—not to me, anyway. I should have been totally focused.

Instead? I was obsessing over Veronica.

To be honest, I'd never stopped. But now it was reaching a crisis point because I had a game to win, a team that was counting on me, and a scholarship to score. Now was not the time to obsess over a girl. Any girl. Not even if that girl was Veronica.

My new friend.

I watched her from across the cafeteria, like I had every day this week. I'd been worried about her on Monday, about how she would deal with the aftermath of the Tina incident. But she'd handled it like a champ. From what I could tell she'd taken the high road. I'd been standing with Alex,

Melody, Tina and a few others on Monday and when she'd walked by she'd given us all that same friendly smile she always wore. The one that was neither ingratiating nor vacant, just...friendly.

I was glad to see that Melody, at least, gave her a wave and a smile like nothing was wrong. Alex and Tina either didn't see her because they were too busy making out or they pretended not to see her.

From what I could tell, Veronica had come out looking like the winner in the scenario. She'd been the mistreated new girl and if anything, she was even more well liked now thanks to the fact that she'd been so poorly treated by Tina, who everyone knew had a tendency to be a mean girl.

I'd split from the group to walk with her. I hadn't wanted her to be alone on her first day back, and she gave me a grateful look before plastering that friendly smile on her face. We'd chatted for a bit about our weekends and it was all very... friendly.

Because that's what we were. Friends.

Somehow that felt anti-climactic. No, not just anti-climactic. It felt *wrong*. Did I want to be friends with her? Hell yes. Of course I did. She was the first person in this school that I felt a connection to. She was the first person I'd opened up to since April and Lee screwed me over last year.

So, yeah, obviously I wanted to be friends. But did I *just* want to be friends? I watched her walk into the cafeteria and head straight toward the table in the back where she'd been sitting this week with some girls I recognized from the soccer team.

She seemed to laugh more now that she was sitting with them. And I saw her get animated as she was talking. When she was sitting with Melody and the others she'd been more prone to sit quietly and listen, smiling and laughing politely, rather than genuinely.

And all this begged the question—just how long had I been watching her like this? Man, I was creeping myself out with my stalker ways. I hadn't even realized I'd been paying such close attention to Veronica's lunch habits until now.

Now, the question I'd been asking myself since Monday afternoon seemed to echo through my brain. Did I really want to be *just friends* with Veronica Smith?

She slid into the bench seat and her face lit up with a grin at something one of her new friends said. I felt that smile like she'd reached into my chest and squeezed.

No. The answer was clear and there was no use trying to deny it to myself any longer. I didn't want to just be friends with Veronica. And I didn't want to just hookup with her either.

I wanted to be with her. For real.

I sat there staring at her for who knows how long before Alex interrupted. "Yo, earth to Drew."

Turning to face him, I met all kinds of weird looks from my teammates. "You all right, man?" Alex asked.

I nodded. "Yeah. Just thinking about the game tonight."

Lie. But it was an effective lie. Everyone at the table nodded in understanding. This was a big game. *The* game. Everyone knew the pressure I was under so they left me alone for the remainder of lunch. I was free to stare and obsess to my heart's content.

I couldn't believe it. Oh, I'd finally reconciled the fact that Ronnie and Veronica were one and the same. I was no longer blown away by the knowledge that they were two sides of the same person, but I was still marveling over the fact that I had a thing for her.

For Ronnie. Having a thing for Veronica wasn't so strange, but Ronnie? This was the girl who beat up Tommy Landon when he'd picked on one of her friends. If I was being honest, I'd never really thought of her as a girl before. I'd thought of her as Ronnie, asexual at best. I could vividly remember the baseball caps she wore and the oversized jerseys and tees.

I think we all thought of her as one of the boys. But looking at her now across the room, it was hard to see how we could have missed the beauty who was in our midst that whole time. I'd noticed that since the Tina debacle she seemed to have eased up on the girly. She wasn't sporting heels in the hall and she'd been wearing jeans instead of sundresses.

She still looked hot, don't get me wrong. But she looked a little more like her old self.

Granted, I don't think I ever saw Ronnie wearing skinny jeans or flattering, figure-forming tops. But even so, it was hard to believe we hadn't seen past the clothes and hairstyles. I mean, how had I missed that smile? How had I not seen the way it transformed her face and made her radiant?

Maybe she'd been right. Maybe she had become invisible, in a way. I guess when you grew up with someone and saw them every single day, it was easy to take them for granted.

I found myself smiling like an idiot as she laughed at something her friends said, her head tipping back and her eyes screwed up tight in unselfconscious abandon.

I never wanted to take Veronica Smith for granted again. She deserved so much more than being invisible or treated to the games and manipulations of the Tina and Alex's of this world.

She deserved to be treated right. To be taken out on a

proper date—one that included dinner. She deserved to be seen and heard and freakin' cherished.

Yeah, okay, maybe I was a bit of a romantic deep down. That was one of the reasons I'd sworn off dating after April. Because I know myself and I know that I can't keep my distance. I have a hard time compartmentalizing.

Like right now. I should be focused on the game, but it was impossible to do until I straightened this out with Veronica.

I thought about that all throughout lunch, and when the bell rang signaling the end of lunch, I knew what I had to do.

I was going to ask her out. Right away. No waiting. It might be crazy to start dating again, but not doing something about these feelings was just as distracting. Maybe even more distracting. If I didn't do something about this infatuation soon, I would never be able to stop thinking about her. At least if she said yes, I'd have some sort of resolution. I could focus on the game and on our trophy.

Really, when all was said and done, I was doing this for the sake of my team.

Me and my noble reasons headed over to her table. I caught her just as she came to stand, picking up the remains of her bagged lunch and crumbling it in a ball to throw away.

Her smile grew as she spotted me. "Hey, Remi."

Her use of my last name was so very friendly it almost threw me off my mission. Her friends looked surprised by my sudden appearance at their table as they gathered their bags to head out. I got more than a couple questioning looks. If there was one thing I didn't particularly need at the moment, it was an audience.

I nodded toward the hallway. "Walk you to your next class?"

"Sure," she said with a nod, falling into step next to me. "So, you nervous about the game tonight?"

I nodded because it was partially true. I was nervous, but not so much about the game as I was about asking her out. When I thought about the game I felt the same adrenaline rush I always got—more of a thrill of excitement than nerves.

But asking out Veronica Smith? Or Ronnie, for that matter?

My palms were officially sweating.

"Are you going tonight?" I asked.

She shot me a look. "Of course. I wouldn't miss it."

A warmth flooded my muscles at the sweet sincerity in her voice. "Cool."

Yup, cool. That was me, Mr. Eloquence.

"Do you have any plans for afterward?" I shoved my hands in my pocket. This was harder than I'd thought it would be. Why couldn't I just spit out the words, *will you go out with me*? Instead I found myself circling the question like a wuss.

She shrugged, sidestepping a student who was in her path. "I heard everyone was going to the Hamilton Diner afterward to celebrate."

"Or commiserate," I added automatically. Not because I was being pessimistic but because when it came to big games, one could never be too careful about getting too cocky. Or being jinxed. And yes, I was superstitious about stuff like that. It might not make sense, but there it was.

She looked in my direction with arched brows. "Oh please. You're going to kill it tonight. I've seen you play."

"You have?" Her words got me even further off track. I was supposed to be focusing on asking her out but my stupid ego couldn't resist hearing more.

"Of course." She picked up her pace and I had to hustle to stay next to her. When I glanced over, I could have sworn she was blushing.

Ronnie didn't blush, did she? Maybe Veronica did.

Okay, I really had to stop thinking about her as two different people. She was still the same girl I'd always known, just...different. Or not different and I was the one who'd changed.

Huh. That thought temporarily distracted me from what she was saying and I only caught the tail end.

"...everyone from Atwater was at the last game of the season when you struck out their player in overtime." She turned to me with a grin that made me feel a million feet tall. "That was epic."

Epic. I liked that. My ego freakin' loved it.

I had to be careful or I'd start strutting like a cocky moron. It wasn't just the praise. I mean, I was the star of the school's baseball team. Not to brag, but I got a lot of praise, from guys and girls alike. And parents, and teachers, and some local business owners... Praise I was used to.

But praise from Veronica?

It was a heady experience.

I cleared my throat as I summoned up the nerve to ask her out like a man. Before I could, she spun to face me with an expectant look. "So I guess I'll see you at the diner tonight after the game, right?"

My mouth opened and I couldn't think of how to respond. Yes? But also no. That's not what I meant. I didn't want to hang out with Veronica and Melody and Alex and the rest of the student body population who would all be there, celebrating or commiserating.

I wanted to be alone with her.

But before I could piece together the right words to say any of that, I realized two things at once. We'd reached Veronica's classroom and her question had been rhetorical. She wasn't waiting for an answer, she was already turning away from me, heading toward class.

"Wait, Veronica, I—"

She paused in the doorway, turning back to face me. But a handful of other students were trying to squeeze past her and our little bubble was shattered as one of the girls said something to her and someone else called out good luck to me in the hallway.

My chance was over. I'd missed my opportunity.

But I had to say something; she was waiting for me to speak. I swallowed down my disappointment. There would be other chances, better moments.

"I, uh...I'm glad you're coming to the game tonight."

Her warm, kind gaze met mine and I had a brief moment of hope that she would understand what I meant by that. For a second I thought she did read more into that stupid comment, but then she gave me another friendly smile. "Of course I'll be there to support you. That's what friends do."

She gave me a cute little wink before turning and walking in without a second glance.

That's what friends do? Right. Because we were friends and, as far as Veronica was concerned, that was all we were.

I bit back a groan as I fought past a tide of students who were rushing to beat the next bell signaling the start of class. I took my time, not only because I would already be late to my next class on the other side of the building but because today was one of those days where it was good to be the star pitcher of a winning baseball team.

Not even the strictest teacher would punish me for being late today of all days.

So I took my time and thought over what I should have said. What I *would* say the very next time I had the chance.

NINE

Veronica

I SHIFTED on the bleacher seat next to Trent. "Have I mentioned that I owe you?"

Baseball was boring, according to Trent. Most sports were boring to this computer nerd, yet he gamely attended my soccer tournaments to support me. But going to a high school baseball game for a sport he didn't even like? This was going above and beyond.

He grinned, leaning over to nudge me with his shoulder. "You can pay me back by not talking about hair, makeup, or clothes for the duration of this game. Think you can handle that?"

I let out short laugh at the totally accurate criticism. Most of the time Trent was around, so was Margo, which meant that the conversation had a tendency to steer toward my makeover. More specifically, how I was going to maintain the look and not destroy all of Margo's hard work.

"Hey, it's not my fault your girlfriend has turned my makeover into her charity work for the year."

His huff of laughter was sweet. Even when we were laughing about Margo and her overzealous ways, he got this dopey look on his face. The way he looked when Margo's name was mentioned—that's what I wanted.

I didn't just want a first kiss, or a date with some random guy like Alex… I wanted *this*. The real deal. I wanted a boyfriend who looked just as dopey as Trent did whenever Margo was around. I wanted a real relationship.

And I wanted it with Drew.

Ugh. Get over it already. Nearly a week had passed since Drew's heroic rescue but there was no sign of these feelings fading. Maybe my expectations had been too high, but I'd hoped I'd have moved on from this stupid crush by now.

Not only had the crush not faded away like I'd hoped, it had somehow managed to grow. I'm pretty sure I was in full-blown infatuation territory here.

"So tell me again what we're doing here?" Trent asked as he reached over to steal some of the fries I'd bought at the concession stand. "I thought you'd given up on trying to befriend those jerks who humiliated you."

I nodded. "I have."

He turned to face me with an expectant look. "So what are we doing here then?"

I spotted the group of jerks in question down near the bottom of the bleachers. From this far up, it was easy to believe they were as nice, fun, and beautiful as they appeared when I'd first met them.

Unfortunately for them, I got to know them. There was nothing nice or fun about that group. The more I learned from hanging out with normal girls, like my new friends on the soccer team, that crowd was synonymous with backstabbing and vicious gossip.

I guess I'd been lucky to figure that out when I had. At least I'd managed to walk away from them with my soul intact. I was still friendly in the hallways but I'd kept my distance, and I didn't exactly hear anyone crying about it on their end either.

I turned away from that group and faced my friend. My *real* friend. "I'm here to support Drew." I nudged his shoulder like he'd nudged mine. "And you're here to support me."

He let out a long suffering sigh. "So...what? You and Drew Remi are friends now?"

I hadn't told him about the bonding talk we'd had over pizza so his confusion was warranted. I shrugged. "I guess."

Part of me was just as confused by this new arrangement as Trent was. But, at the same time, after the way he'd opened up to me, I wanted to be a friend to him. Hottie or not, star pitcher or not—he was a good guy. A nice guy.

Surprisingly sweet, really.

And he was funny and smart, and really easy to be around when I could manage to forget how hot he was and stop doing stupid things like blushing around him.

Man, blushing sucked. The weirdest things seemed to set it off around him. Heat would flood my cheeks with no notice just because he looked at me too closely or gave me a smile that felt too intimate for "just friends."

But me and my blushing would get over it. It wasn't going to happen and once my brain thoroughly registered that information, Drew and I would be friends.

Just friends.

And until then?

I watched Drew run out onto the field and take the

mound. Holy hell, he was too hot for life. My heartrate sped up just watching him in all his uniformed glory.

Until then I would fake it till I made it. Just like my popularity project, I could fake being friends with Drew until my feelings toward him settled into the friend zone, where they belonged.

I watched in awe and one hundred percent female appreciation as Drew worked his magic. The guy wasn't a local baseball star for nothing—he had moves. He looked like such a natural out there, it took my breath away.

Every few minutes I'd have to remind myself that we were just friends. My new rule of thumb to live by? Friends don't drool over other friends.

It wasn't exactly a great slogan on par with "say no to drugs" or "just do it" but it suited my needs at this particular moment.

My brain could grasp the concept of friendship, but my body and heart were so not on board. "This sucks," I muttered at one point after having to remind myself yet again that ogling a guy's butt as he ran off the field was *not* acceptable friend behavior.

"What sucks?" Trent asked.

I heaved a heavy sigh. "Where do you stand on boy talk?"

I felt his side eye. Or maybe I just knew him well enough to know that my question warranted one of *those* looks. "It depends," he said slowly. This was new terrain for both of us. "Who's the boy?"

I bit my lip. This was harder than I'd thought. It was bad enough hearing him talk about Margo like that and she was his girlfriend. But I needed help. Bad. And Margo was nowhere to be seen. Even if she was, she wouldn't be a help. She was such a romantic, her advice would be clouded in rose-colored glasses. I didn't need optimistic hope right now, I needed a cold dose of realism. Maybe Trent could talk some sense into my heart and body because my brain clearly wasn't up to the task.

I swallowed down the uncomfortable feeling and kept my eyes trained on the field. "You're looking at him."

Drew had just resumed his position and Trent groaned beside me. "You too?"

I knew what he meant. It had been a joke for years that every girl at Atwater was gaga for Drew Remi.

Everyone but me.

And Margo, presumably. Hopefully. But judging by the way she'd swooned every time I mentioned him, I could safely say she understood his sex appeal even if she wasn't outright crushing herself.

"I know, it's ridiculous," I said with a shake of my head. I mean, of course it was ridiculous. He was Drew freakin' Remi—popular, hot, sexy, sweet, and the guy who could have any girl ever, and didn't. Ever. Not since April. He'd been the first to admit that he doesn't date anymore so why would he break that rule now? And for me? His friend?

"It is ridiculous," Trent said.

My heart fell just a little bit further toward the crumbs and peanut shells on the ground at our feet.

"You could do so much better." Trent stuck one of my fries in his mouth and continued watching the game. He didn't laugh, didn't smirk. He didn't do or say anything to make me think he might be kidding.

Still, I stared at him, waiting for him to crack up. "You're kidding, right?"

He turned to face me. "What?"

"You're kidding," I told him.

"No, I'm not." He looked honestly confused.

"Every girl wants Drew."

His brow furrowed even more. He was staring at me like I'd just started speaking Klingon. "So?"

"*So?*" I repeated. But my *so* was louder and far more irritated.

He let out a sharp exhale in obvious exasperation. "So," he drawled. "He obviously doesn't want *every* girl, so what does that matter?"

I opened my mouth to argue and then slammed it shut. He didn't want *every* girl. I'm sure he didn't want *any* girl, either, just like I didn't want any guy.

I couldn't protest because he had a point.

Dammit. I hated when he had a point. Particularly when it meant he was right and I was wrong.

But I wasn't totally wrong. "But he still doesn't want me."

He eyed me again, this time with a clearly critical eye like he was sizing me up from an objective point of view. "How do you know?"

"Because we're friends," I said, imbuing the word friends with all the disgust I could muster. "He said so."

Trent was starting to get a little smirk that made me want to smack him. "You know, sometimes friendships become more. I'd even go so far as to say that friendship is kind of crucial to the whole love thing."

"Love?" My voice sounded snarky out of habit. "Who said anything about love?"

He rolled his eyes. "All I'm saying is that relationships usually start off with people liking each other." He tilted his chin down and gave me a 'you're an idiot so I'll spell it out for you' look. "Which means…friends."

Huh. I turned back and faced the field, watching Drew

be amazing and trying not to let my hopes out of their ironclad cage as I pondered what Trent had said.

When Trent spoke again, he startled me. I'd like to say I was in the midst of having some super insightful deep thoughts, but really I'd just caught myself drooling again.

Bad Ronnie. Bad!

"So what kind of girl is he looking for?" Trent asked.

"What?" I spun to face him, swiping the side of my mouth just in case. "Drew?"

He smirked again and this time I did smack his arm. "Yeah, Drew. That's who you have a crush on, right?"

I scowled at him. His teasing tone was beyond obnoxious and I was starting to regret I'd ever said anything.

"Well?" he prompted. "What kind of girl is he looking for?"

"He's not looking for anyone," I said. "That's the point. He was burned before and he's tired of the drama. He's sick of people playing games..." I trailed off with a shrug.

Trent stared at me for a minute and I could see his brain working. He gave me an irritatingly mysterious smile before turning back to the field. "Well then I guess you're right. You're out of the running."

"What do you mean by that?" Of course, I knew exactly what he meant by that. "You think I play games? I don't play games."

He turned to look at me and my outrage faltered. "Except for *Mario Kart*. And *Fallout 4* and...you know what I mean."

His gaze was so knowing. Unbearably knowing. The kind of knowing that only a best friend of forever could manage.

I turned away and looked at the field but this time I wasn't paying attention to the game, or the pitcher, or even the pitcher's superfine butt. I wanted to summon up anger at his words but they hit a nerve.

Had I been playing games?

I turned back to Trent and he gave me a look that was the very definition of tough love. "Admit it, Ronnie, you've been playing games this whole time with the *new and improved Veronica* thing." He donned a remarkably spot-on impersonation of me when he'd said that and I gave him a grudging smile.

Very grudging, because his words stung. But how much they stung clued me in to the fact that they held merit.

I might not be the most self aware person in the world, but I wasn't totally blind to my faults, either. Still, I felt the need to justify my mentality. His criticism felt too harsh. "I haven't been playing games," I said.

He didn't argue with me but his tone didn't alter either. It was smug and annoyingly wise. "But you have been playing a role."

"That's not the same thing," I said.

He arched one brow. Could it talk, that single expressive eyebrow would have said, *Close enough*.

I straightened in my seat and looked around the crowd, suddenly acutely aware of where we were and who was around us. My new classmates. The ones who knew me as Veronica, and all that name implied.

"This new me," I said, gesturing to my jeans and T-shirt that actually fit. "This isn't some act, Trent. It's me." I met his gaze and wouldn't let him look away. This felt important for some reason. To our friendship, maybe, and definitely to me. "This is me, just not the me you're used to."

He looked agitated as he shook his head and scratched the back of his neck. His confusion was apparent. "It's not you, Ronnie. It's an act."

Fake it til you make it. "Maybe at first," I admitted. "At first it was me being the person I wanted to be."

He raised his brows in unspoken challenge and I rolled my eyes. He was such a stickler for honesty. "Fine, maybe it was the person I wanted other people to see."

"You wanted to fit in."

"Yeah," I snapped. "I wanted to fit in."

He'd said it as a challenge. An accusation, even. But I wasn't ashamed and I didn't want to be. I was officially sick of him judging me for wanting something different in life. Of wanting to *be* something different.

I knew why it made him uncomfortable and I got it. But that didn't mean I had to go along with it. This was my life and I'd be damned if his discomfort was going to affect the way I lived it.

But, even as I thought those empowering thoughts, his criticism bugged me. I hated the hint of truth to it. For my own sake more than his, I found myself rationalizing and explaining. "It wasn't just about popularity and boys, even though that was part of it. I just wanted to show people a different side of me. I've been pigeonholed for so long as the class tomboy." I shook my head, hating the emotion in my voice that made us both discomfort. "I hated being invisible. An asexual non-entity to the guys and a nobody loser who had nothing in common with the rest of the girls in our class."

"You had us." He said it softly, simply, and it made me feel like the crumbs and garbage at our feet.

It was what Margo had said about how she was my friend except worse. A million times worse because Trent had been by my side forever. He and the guys always had my back and kept me company. We were there for each other...and Trent thought that wasn't good enough.

"I know I had you guys, and I loved that," I said. "I *love* that."

"But?"

When I didn't say anything he answered for me. "But you wanted more than that. More than us."

"Yes," I said. At his hurt look, I hurried to add, "Not to the more than you part. Ugh, don't be melodramatic."

"Fine, but you did want more. What we had wasn't enough."

"Not anymore, no." I watched as his expression grew hurt, painfully close to a wounded puppy dog. I couldn't take it. I was making a mess of this explanation but I needed him to understand. "This wasn't about you. It was about me."

He shook his head. "And it was important to you that people buy into this new version of you. Yeah, I get it."

But he didn't, that much was clear in his tone.

I stared down at my cute little wedge heels that might not have been as comfortable as my sneakers but I'd opted for them anyway. I wished absently that they might have the answers within their cute silver straps. And in a way, I realized, they did. "Look at these wedges."

I could feel his stare on the side of my face. He was probably looking at me like I was nuts. I half expected to him to question why now of all times I wanted his input on my footwear.

Instead, he asked, "What the hell are wedges?"

I let out short laugh before I could stop it. "They're my shoes, idiot. Look at them."

I heard him sigh but when I glanced over he was looking. "Well?" I asked. "What do you think?"

His gaze turned weary. "Seriously? Now you want to

talk about how your shoes look? I'm not Margo, Ronnie. I don't care."

"Well I do, and that's exactly my point."

Now he definitely stared at me like I'd lost my mind. "What point?"

"Maybe at first I was playing a role," I said. "And maybe that's weird, I don't know. But it wasn't just about being popular and all that crap."

"Oh no?"

"No," I said a little too loudly. But really, his judgy tone was annoying the hell out of me. "I was trying to figure myself out. I still am."

He jerked back a bit. "What does that even mean?"

"It means I've changed," I said. "It means I've been changing. We all have."

"I haven't."

I scoffed at that, and when he gave me a haughty look that made me want to scream, I spelled it out. "You really don't think you've changed?" I crossed my arms. "Or maybe you just thought I hadn't noticed."

"I have *not*—"

"You have a girlfriend."

"That's not changing, I—"

"You took her to see *Disney on Ice*."

He clamped his mouth shut. Then his expression turned sheepish. "She told you about that, huh?"

"Yeah. And it's cool." I stopped and backtracked. "Well, it's not cool. Nothing about Ice Capades is cool."

He smirked and for the first time in what felt like ages that heavy feeling in my chest lifted a bit. "But it's sweet," I said. "What you did for her. And it's cool that you've gone outside of your comfort zone to make her happy."

He stared at me for a moment, his gaze dropping to my

clothes and those uncomfortable but oddly empowering wedges. "And this is you going out of your comfort zone?"

"Yes." I hesitated. "Well, maybe not totally. Not at first. But it *is* me changing and figuring out who I want to be."

He shifted beside me and I knew he was thinking. I let him think.

"Why wasn't Ronnie good enough?" He half turned to face me again. "The old Ronnie, I mean. The not-better version, but the version we all loved."

I glanced over at his use of the past tense and he rolled his eyes. "The version we *love*."

I sighed because honestly words were hard to come by. It was hard enough to understand myself let alone explain it to someone who was critical about it. "Because I outgrew her." I shifted on the bleacher. No, that wasn't right. "I became more than her."

Turning to face him, I threw another fry in my mouth and talked while I chewed, because this was Trent and I could be rude like that with him. "I still love playing videogames and playing soccer," I said. "I don't particularly enjoy the girlie stuff, unless it's with Margo, because she's cool and she doesn't seem to care when I don't know what she's talking about."

He waited as I took a deep breath. "But I also like being seen. And I don't mean being popular, I mean being noticed. Being recognized at school and not just on the playing field."

I stared down at the fries. "I like not only being known for one thing, if I'm recognized for anything at all. I like being able to try a new look or a new hairstyle or a new hobby or new interests..." I let my babbling trail off. "I like starting fresh and being able to be anyone I want to be."

I looked over at him. "I'm not totally sure who this new Veronica is yet, but she will always include Ronnie."

He stared at me for a minute before grinning. "Will this new Veronica continue to talk about herself in the third person?"

I laughed and the laughter felt so good. The fact that he was smiling a genuine smile made me want to laugh and cry at once. "Maybe," I said. "Who knows what Veronica will do?"

"Oh God, Margo's created a monster," he said.

For a second there, life was good again. Me and Trent were on the same page, something we hadn't been since school started. And me and Drew?

I could see him on the sidelines, watching the other team's hitter at bat with a couple other guys from the team. Everything Trent had said about me and playing games... now I knew why it had made me feel off. He had struck a nerve, but it wasn't because I was ashamed of wanting to try different clothes or hang out with new people. It was because with Drew, I had played games.

"You were right," I said. When he looked over in surprise, I added, "Sort of."

"Oh yeah, how was I sort of right?"

"I wasn't being honest with Drew at the start. You know, when I was pretending not to know who he was because he didn't know who I was and then he didn't—"

"Yeah, I get it." Trent held up a hand to shut me up. "I was there for the whole will-he-won't-he-remember thing. Don't need a play-by-play."

"Right," I said. "Sorry." Then I shrugged. "I'm just saying, that whole thing wasn't me."

At his arched brow, I added. "It's not the old me and it's not the new me either. I was playing games and I hate that."

He nodded and it suddenly felt like I was in a confessional. "He deserves better than that, you know? After the crap he's been through this past year, he deserves a girl who doesn't play games."

Trent studied me for a while. "Then it sounds like you know what you have to do."

I turned back to the field and watched Drew be awesome. I knew what he was going to say but I didn't want to hear it, so I played dumb instead. "I do?" My grudging tone gave me away.

"You do," he said. "You know you have to be honest with him. If it's not just friendship you want than you should tell him."

I turned to face Drew. "But what if we're not there yet?" I asked. "What if you're right about starting out as friends and—"

"I didn't say you had to tell him today," he said, interrupting me again with another hand in the face.

Seriously, the guy was asking for a smackdown. But, since he was currently the only one in our little group who was in a healthy, nauseatingly happy relationship, I supposed I had to swallow down my irritation and accept that he spoke the truth.

Besides, his truth made me feel a whole lot more relaxed, like I'd just gotten a "get out of jail free" card or something. He was right, I didn't have to tell him today, or even tomorrow.

"You do have to tell him eventually though," Trent said.

I nodded. "Yeah, I get it."

"At the very least you need to spend time with him," said Trent, the suddenly self-proclaimed Love Doctor. "You need to see where it goes."

I murmured something in agreement. I was ready to

drop this topic now that I'd decided to press pause on the crazy and just let things progress naturally.

But apparently Trent was on a roll. "And don't discount yourself right off the bat just because you don't think you're what he wants."

I turned to find him eyeing me again from head to toe. "Trust me, you're what a lot of guys want."

"Ew."

He looked as disgusted as I felt as he held his hands up. "Not me, obviously."

"Still ew."

"But some guys—"

"Just stop talking," I said.

"Right." He turned back to the field. "So...Good game, huh?"

I glanced over at the scoreboard. We were still winning. "Yeah, great game."

TEN

Drew

OUR TEAM HAD CRUSHED the competition. It was a great game. An epic win. My adrenaline had me riding a high after the game and it showed no signs of abating even now as I drove my jointly shared clunker to the diner where the rest of the school would be waiting.

Well, maybe not the whole school, but a lot of it.

And Veronica. She would be there.

That was why my adrenaline was still pumping. This was it. No more procrastinating. I was going to inform her that I'd been wrong before about being friends.

No, that didn't sound right. I did want to be friends, but I also wanted to be more than that, too.

But what if I screwed everything up by telling her that?

That was a risk I was just going to have to take, I decided as I slammed the car door shut behind me. I smiled and waved to the students and team family members who shouted out to me as I walked into the diner. Apparently the wait was a long one if crowds of people were mingling outside waiting for a table.

The team would have one reserved though—or at least, some nice friends and family would have made sure one was free for us, since the diner didn't exactly do reservations, just like it didn't do hors d'oeuvres or cocktails. It was a diner, in the most classic sense of the term. All the food was greasy, the silverware was dirty, and the menus looked like they hadn't been changed out since the Reagan administration.

I searched the crowd as I walked in, trying to spot Veronica without being too impolite to the people who were trying to talk to me.

No Veronica. I tried not to be too disappointed. I mean, this diner was hardly the romantic spot of my dreams to be asking a girl out.

Especially not a girl who I really liked. I spotted Alex waving to me from a table in the back and gave him a nod. Then I continued to look around even as I slowly made my way back there.

I was stalling. I was totally, lamely stalling because I didn't want Veronica to come in and see me with the people who were mean to her. And I didn't want to have to make my excuses to a group of people so I could run to her side the moment she appeared...

So yeah, I was totally stalling.

The stalling paid off. There she was, at a little corner table—barely a table at all. Her head was bent over a menu and she was nearly hidden by the cascade of hair that fell in front of her face.

I headed in her direction even as my jealous gaze latched onto the guy sitting across from her. Tall and lanky, he had shaggy hair and a T-shirt with some band logo.

He looked about as out of place here surrounded by these baseball players and cheerleaders as I'd probably look if I went to a heavy metal show.

Who the hell was this? Had she brought a *date* to *my* game?

That was just all sorts of wrong. Granted, she might not have understood what I'd meant when I'd asked if she was coming tonight, but that was beside the point. An angry possessiveness had me picking up my pace, weaving around people and ignoring their attempts to talk to me.

She was mine.

I don't know how this happened and I can't explain why. All I knew in that moment was the acute, almost panicky realization that she was mine. At least, I wanted her to be. Just like I wanted to be hers.

I'd never felt like this before. Not even with April. Definitely not with April.

This went beyond having a crush or being attracted. This was like friendship plus longing plus attraction... It was intense.

I didn't even notice anyone else in the diner. All I could see was Veronica and her date. I needed to get to her, talk to her. I had to make her see that I cared about her and that we belonged together.

And I had to do it now, before it was too late.

I sidestepped a senior who was blocking my path in the crowded aisle and took another step in their direction. As I did, the guy at her table lifted his head and looked in my direction.

Trent Burton.

I stopped in my tracks for one second as relief washed over me. Trent, Ronnie Smith's best friend. Maybe I wasn't too late, after all.

Thank God.

A waitress trying to get past me brought me back to reality and I headed toward them again, studiously ignoring the shouts from Alex, Tina, and some others I had no interest in talking to.

Trent spotted me and nudged Veronica. She looked up at him and then over to me.

She smiled. I don't think it would be overkill to say that time stopped in that moment. Her smile was everything. It was sweet and teasing and shy and confident... it was everything I loved about Veronica.

It was strength and vulnerability, it was refreshing honesty and a sharp kick in the ass, it was uncertainty about her own beauty, but an innate confidence that was sexy as hell. It was genuine and pure, and a complete and utter lack of insincerity.

I freakin' loved that smile.

I loved it so much I finally stopped overthinking. I stopped worrying about how she would respond, and I manned up.

Coming to stand by her table, I met her smile and nodded toward the front entrance, where a group of people clogged the doorway. "Can we talk for a sec?"

Oh man. There was something so freeing about saying those words. This time I wouldn't choke. This time I would spit it out.

Will you go out with me?

Maybe it was the post-win buzz but I had the kind of confidence that could make a man fly. I could sure as hell ask out the girl of my dreams. She cast a quick glance to Trent, who I nodded to as well to avoid being rude. But honestly, I had no time for playing catch-up with a former classmate. I had to do this while I still had the nerve.

He didn't do much of anything in return, just stared at me like I was from another planet or something. Apparently Veronica took his silence as an okay because she got up and led the way toward the exit.

All eyes were on us, but it couldn't be helped. Well, it could. But that would mean putting this off even longer and that was not something I was willing to do. She sort of hesitated halfway toward the door, turning back to give me a questioning look but I just shoved my hands into my pockets and nodded toward the door.

She turned to keep walking but it was obvious she was confused, and who could blame her? I was the one who'd spelled it out that I'd wanted to be friends. So why did I need alone time with her now when I was supposed to be hanging with my teammates?

My mind went back to the weekend before—more specifically the conversation we'd had as she'd inhaled her pizza.

I could kick myself now for how much I'd told her. She must think I was some commitment-phobe. Or maybe she thought I was still heartbroken over April.

Somehow I needed to explain to her that I wasn't still hung up on April and I don't think I was ever really heartbroken. Hurt? Yeah. Her timing had sucked, and so had her inconsiderate choice of guys to move on with. Lee was just as much to blame for that one. But heartbroken? No. I would have had to have been in love to have a broken heart and I'd never loved April.

It was too soon to say I loved Veronica, but I knew without a doubt that what I felt for her already was on a whole different level than anything I'd felt before.

That thought made me nervous. For the first time since

the game ended, my rush of adrenaline-fueled confidence faltered.

I liked her too much. How was I supposed to explain all this? Words had never been my strong suit. I was an action man. I was physical, not philosophical. I didn't know the first thing about saying romantic things or—

She came to a stop outside the door to the diner and I bumped into her from behind. Clearly I wasn't even physically capable around her. Man, this thing I felt around her was messing with my head in a major way if I couldn't even walk properly.

She gave me another questioning look as she crossed her arms and huddled in on herself.

It was a typical fall night, brisk and windy now that the sun had set. She was only wearing a T-shirt and I slipped off my jacket and handed it to her.

"Thanks." She shrugged into it before tilting her head to the side in a silent question. *What are we doing out here?*

There were still too many people around, and no one would leave me alone. Voices kept calling out to me. *Hey man. Good game, Drew. You da man, dawg.*

I grabbed her hand and pulled her around a corner so we were out of sight. Only then could I breathe easily. This would be hard enough without an audience.

"Are you okay?" she asked.

I nodded. "Yeah, I, uh—" Oh hell, I should have planned out a speech beforehand. "Remember last weekend when we were talking over pizza?"

She nodded and I could see confusion in her eyes. Where exactly was I going with this?

Excellent question. Once again I was doing a phenomenal job of beating around the bush. I tried to focus. I needed her to understand that I no longer had those hangups, not when it came to her.

"I said some stuff... I mean, I know I told you about my ex and—" Ah hell. I was no good at talking.

Her eyes widened in surprise as I cursed under my breath. Then I reached out to her, pulled her close, and kissed her.

She was warm and wonderful in my arms. That clean citrus scent overwhelmed me and the feel of her body pressed against mine was more perfect than I could ever have imagined. Her lips were soft and lush beneath mine.

But she was frozen, a statue in my arms.

After a moment of stunned stillness, she responded. Hesitantly at first, but oh so sweetly. Her lips moved against mine and I couldn't hold back. The rest of the world disappeared as I kissed her with everything I had. This was just about her and me, and everything I was trying to tell her that I couldn't say with words.

I like you. I want to be with you.

Her lean, perfect body fitted against me like we were made to come together like this. She wrapped her arms around my neck and I tightened my grip on her waist.

If I could, I would never let go.

She felt amazing. Even better than I'd dreamt. And if I was being honest, I'd been dreaming about this moment since Veronica Smith fell into my arms that first day of school.

Her lips were sweet and warm beneath mine, and she met each kiss with the same intensity and passion. She felt it too, just like I knew she would.

Well, I hadn't *known* she would, but I'd hoped. I was lost in the moment, my every sense focused on Veronica—the way she felt pressed against me, the way she made those sweet little moaning sounds in the back of her throat as the kiss grew more intense.

When a car door slammed next to us I barely noticed. "Wow, way to put on a show."

It wasn't until that familiar voice spoke right next to us that I drew back from Veronica in shock. Veronica gazed up at me with wide startled eyes at the interruption.

No, it couldn't be.

I turned to find April and a couple of her friends getting out of a car nearby. She wore a calculating smirk that I knew well.

My stomach fell as I realized that not only was my ex here, but she was looking for trouble.

I felt Veronica's arms untangle from around my neck as she pulled back from me. I wanted to stop her. I didn't want to lose that connection. Not yet, not until we'd had a chance to talk.

But she was turning away from me, watching April and the others as they drew near.

"Don't stop on my account," April said. Her eyes were firmly fixed on me, and for that I was glad. I could deal with April, but I didn't want Veronica to have to.

I held on to Veronica's hand, even though she didn't return my grip. If anything, she seemed to be trying to tug away from me.

April was right next to us and her smirk was knowing, her gaze filled with unpleasant laughter. "Although," she said slowly, teasingly. "Something tells me that whole performance was for my benefit."

She continued to ignore Veronica as she leaned in to me, her hand on my arm as she leaned against me like we were still a couple. "You saw us pull up, am I right?"

It took me a second to understand what she meant. She

thought I'd been kissing Veronica to get back at her. That I was trying to make her jealous or something.

I shook my head. Of all the egotistical, ridiculous—

"I'd better go." Veronica twisted her hand out from mine and started backing away.

When I met her gaze, my heart fell into the pit of my stomach.

No. No, no, no. This could not be happening. She couldn't actually believe that I'd done that to—

"Veronica, don't go," I called out, not caring that April and her friends were watching us with avid interest.

Veronica's steps faltered as her eyes locked with mine.

"Veronica," April repeated, openly assessing Veronica like she was a bug under a magnifying glass. "Wait a second...*Ronnie?*"

April's voice was filled with unkind laughter as she turned to her giggling friends. "Ronnie Smith?" She whirled around to face me. "You were kissing *Ronnie Smith?*"

Their laughter was cruel and I saw the hurt and humiliation that was written all over Veronica's face. I needed to make this right, but I had no idea how.

"Veronica," I said, but when I took a step in her direction, she spun around and walked away from me.

ELEVEN

Veronica

I FOUND Trent exactly where I'd left him. "We've got to go."

He frowned up at me. "What's wrong?"

I shook my head. I couldn't talk. If I did I would cry, and I did not cry. Ever. And I had no plans to start now in front of half the Briarwood junior class. Not even if my heart was breaking.

But that was overkill. Obviously my heart wasn't breaking. We weren't even together. How could I have a broken heart?

Right. Try telling that to gaping hole in my chest where my heart used to be.

I bit my lip to stem a rising tide of tears, but I bit down too hard and that only made it worse because now I was in physical pain in addition to having had my heart ripped out of my chest.

Apparently seeing the extent of my distress, Trent

grabbed his bag, snatched some money out of his pocket and threw it onto the table, and led me by my elbow back the way I'd come in.

People were looking at us. I could feel the stares, hear the whispers. Of course they were. Yet again Veronica Smith was the class idiot. This time I hadn't been used by some guy I barely knew to make some drama queen jealous.

Nope. This time it was so much worse. I was so incredibly stupid.

I looked up from the ground to see the door in sight. We were almost there; we'd almost made our escape. But then I heard my name being called.

I walked faster, my head down as I navigated the sea of happy baseball fans. Finally, I reached the parking lot and it wouldn't be an overstatement to say that Trent and I broke into a run.

"Who are we running from?" he panted.

I was the athletic one in this friendship for a reason. Trent couldn't run to the end of the block without getting winded.

"We're not running from anyone," I said. This was a blatant falsehood as I was legitimately running.

The only problem? Drew was athletic too.

Also, he was taller, which meant he had longer legs, and he definitely wasn't wearing wedges. I still say I would have won that race if he didn't have that advantage. But, as it was, he ran in front of me and I was forced to stop or run straight into him.

The only thing that could make this night more painful was to feel his arms around me again. That would be the worst. Why? Because it may have been the best sensation I'd ever felt in my entire life. That embrace, that kiss—that was my first kiss. It was the kiss I'd been waiting a lifetime to experience, and it had exceeded all expectations. It had been perfection. For a little while there, I'd thought we were on the same wavelength. I'd thought he felt the same longing for me that I felt for him. I'd thought I'd felt it in his kiss.

Ugh, what I fool I was.

Drew was breathing heavily and his brow was furrowed. "Why are you running from me?"

I sniffed and looked past him, unwilling to meet his gaze. I spotted Trent hovering nearby, probably unsure whether he should stick around for moral support or give us privacy. He seemed to settle for backtracking to stand inconspicuously by a truck. Far enough that he couldn't hear every word, but close enough that he could come running if I needed him.

Thank God for good friends like Trent.

And screw new friends like Drew. With that thought I lifted my chin, still not meeting his gaze but not cowering either. "I don't run from anyone."

Yup. I was in all out denial mode—first with Trent and now with Drew. But you know what? There's something to be said for the whole fake it til you make it mentality. And right now I needed any help I could get.

If acting like I wasn't crushed meant that I no longer felt like this? I'd act the hell out of this situation. Somebody hand me an Academy Award because I was going to fake it like I'd never faked it before.

"Veronica, I can explain."

"No need." My eyes were trained on a bumper sticker that I could read just over Drew's right shoulder. *Honk if you love cheese!* I focused on that stupid phrase like it held all the answers to the mysteries of the universe.

"What do you mean, *no need*?" He sounded irritated.

Good. I hoped I was ruining his perfect, precious night and whatever awesome plan he'd had to get back at April.

"I mean, I get it." I finally dragged my eyes away from the bumper sticker to meet his gaze. I shouldn't have done it. My heart twisted in my chest at the sight of his earnestness. He looked so upset, so hurt.

But what right did he have to be upset? I was the one who'd been hurt here, dammit.

"What do you mean you get it?" He took a step toward me but I backed away. "Before April showed up, I was trying to tell you—I didn't know how to say it—"

I nodded. I'd figured that out already. It had all made sense when April started talking. At first I'd been too shocked to understand, but then her words clicked and it was all so obvious. He'd been trying to make her jealous.

No, he wasn't an asshole like Alex. He'd tried to tell me that when he'd brought up our pizza conversation. Heck, if he'd had enough time he probably would have asked permission. *Would it be too much trouble to make out with me so I can make April angry?*

But he must have seen her pull up and he didn't have time and so he'd kissed me. He probably thought it was no big deal. *Hey, here's Ronnie—my new, totally platonic friend. She'll be cool with playing the role of my new love interest.*

At least, that's how I assumed it went down in his head. Because, you see, the thing that sucked most about all of this was that I still thought Drew was a good guy. A *nice* guy.

He was a nice guy who thought we were friends.

I cast a quick glance over at Trent as my mind called up our earlier conversation. Maybe he'd been right. Maybe I'd been playing games by going along with this new friendship when I knew that my feelings for him went well beyond friendly. Maybe I should have said something sooner. *I don't want to be friends because I'm afraid I might be falling in love with you, as insane as that sounds.*

But I hadn't said anything. I'd been too chicken to own these feelings. But in my defense, I'd thought I had time. We were just starting to forge this new friendship, and besides, who fell for a guy that quickly? Only me. So I'd waited. I'd held my tongue and let him believe that I was okay with being just friends.

And look where it had gotten me?

Brokenhearted.

There it was. I couldn't try to deny it anymore.

Acknowledging it was an honest-to-God heartbreak that? broke down the last of my defenses. The only thing worse than crying in front of the entire student body? Crying in front of Drew Remi, my first crush, my first kiss, and now? My first heartbreak.

But that was exactly what I did.

I should probably say here and now—I am not a pretty crier. This is one of the reasons I go to great lengths not to cry in front of people. Even when I got hurt on the field I chewed on the inside of my lip until they carted me off to the nurse's station.

Because yeah, maybe I was a tomboy who didn't know the first thing about makeup, but I had some pride. And that pride dictated that no one ever see me with a red, puffy nose, blotchy cheeks and making that awful hiccup sound in my throat.

Yet here I was doing exactly that in front of Drew Remi, sexiest guy alive.

Sometimes life sucked so freakin' hard.

The sobs racked my body and I slapped a hand over my mouth just as Drew pulled me against him. I tried to get away but he held my head to his chest and rubbed my back like I was a child or something.

It felt nice. I didn't want to be soothed by anyone, least of all this guy, but my body had other ideas. I could feel myself melting against him until he was cradling me to him like I was something precious.

Like I was some*one* precious.

"I'm sorry," he said, his tone filled with regret.

That somehow made it worse. Maybe because it made it clear that he knew exactly why I was crying. He was basically admitting that he now knew I liked him and he felt sorry for me. And maybe he felt guilty too, because he'd used me to hurt April, but I still believed deep down that his callous actions hadn't been intentional.

He couldn't have known how I'd truly felt. At least, not until I'd kissed him back. Ugh, how incredibly embarrassing. I stopped trying to pull away from his embrace, grateful that at least he couldn't see my scarlet blush as I remembered my stupidly earnest response to that kiss.

How pathetic. He'd probably expected me to grudgingly go along with it, not kiss him back like my life depended on it. I'd probably come across as overly eager. Desperate, even.

And the worst part was, I had been so happy. I should have known something was off, that kiss had been too good to be true. Being swept up in his arms, having his lips meet mine in a way that felt magical, just like a first kiss should.

It had been overwhelming, and perfect, and real. So very real.

And then it had all turned so surreal as April arrived like a figment of my worst nightmares. Suddenly the perfect moment had become one of the worst moments of my life.

And it was all his fault.

"I'm so sorry," he said again.

I shrugged. I honestly didn't know what to say. It *was* his fault. But then again, maybe it wasn't. I mean, it wasn't like he was a mind reader. How could he have known that I'd gone and fallen for him when I'd agreed to be friends?

He leaned down so his lips were close to my hair, and I could feel his chest reverberate beneath my ear. "I swear I didn't know she was coming tonight."

My lungs lost their ability to draw in air. My stomach leapt up to meet my heart as the meaning of his words registered. He kept talking, apologizing for letting her talk to me like that, for letting her near me at all—but I'd stopped listening.

He hadn't known she was coming.

He hadn't known she was coming?

But... But... What did that mean?

Was he being honest? Yes, he was. I didn't have to think about it. There was nothing disingenuous about Drew. Drew wasn't a liar; he had no reason to lie.

More importantly, he seemed to think that I was upset about April's nastiness. He was still talking and it was clear that he had completely misconstrued my tears. He wasn't trying to make me feel less pitiful for having fallen for him. He was apologizing because he hadn't known April would be there.

He was apologizing on April's behalf. But why? I honestly hadn't given her a second thought. After the whole Tina incident I'd resigned myself to the fact that there were some awful people out there. The only thing I could do was make sure to surround myself with the good ones. Like Trent and Margo...and Drew.

I pushed away from his chest so hard he let out an *oof*,

but it was the only way I could get out of his tight hold. "What do you mean, you didn't know she was coming?"

He stared at me for a second. "I mean, I had no idea she was going to be there. I still don't know what she was doing there."

"April, you mean?"

"Of course I mean April. Who else would I be referring to?" He gave me a look that said I was crazy. And I *felt* crazy. I also felt like I had no idea what was going on here. We were clearly speaking two different languages. I shook my head slightly as he gave me a searching look of confusion.

"You didn't know she was going to be there?" I asked.

"Of course not." His look of confusion turned to irritation. "How could I know she was going to be here?"

I shrugged and pointed out the obvious. "I don't know, maybe she'd texted you or something. Maybe she'd told you she'd planned to come to the after party."

"She didn't," he said.

We stared at each other. As much as my head was scrambling to make sense of this, I got the feeling that his brain was working even harder.

"Wait," he said. "You thought that I *knew* she was coming?"

I didn't nod but I didn't shake my head either. Something about the way he'd asked it made me feel ashamed. Like I'd accused him of kicking puppies or something. I finally settled on a noncommittal shrug.

"Oh my God," he said slowly. "You totally did."

I shrugged again. But then I grew a spine and realized that I had no reason to be on the defensive here. I wasn't the one who'd just pulled him into the middle of ex drama. That had been him.

I placed my hands on my hips and lifted my chin. "Well, if you didn't know she was coming, why did you kiss me?"

He widened his eyes and his face basically called me crazypants even though the word didn't come out of his still-open mouth. "Seriously?"

I nodded, though some of my confidence threatened to waver in the face of his obvious shock.

He threw his hands up. "Because I wanted to!"

I stared. I gaped, actually. Maybe it was even gawking, I don't know. All I know is, I was stunned speechless. He wanted to. It sounded so simple it was almost surreal.

Could that be true? A little voice asked in the back of my brain. *Do we believe him?*

Why would he lie?

Before I could answer any of those questions, or even pose them for him to answer, he turned the cards on me. "What about you?" he asked. "Why did you kiss me back?"

I blinked at him. Despite his answer, I felt too raw. Too exposed. I wasn't certain what was going on and I hated the idea of exposing myself to him any further.

Not physically, obviously. I wasn't about to strip down naked. But I'd be exposing myself emotionally and I wasn't sure I could do that. Because now I knew exactly how much it would hurt if he didn't feel the same.

But what if he did?

But what if he didn't?

I'd just experienced the worst heartbreak of my admittedly short life, and I had no desire to feel that way again...

Although, if I didn't take a chance, if I didn't at least see if there was a possibility for us, would I be able to live with myself? Hadn't I just been kicking myself for not being honest with him sooner? Now I was being given another chance. He hadn't known April would be there. Maybe I hadn't been outright rejected...not yet, at least.

And maybe I wouldn't be at all. Maybe he felt the same. I looked into his eyes and wished that the answer was clear. But it wasn't. All I saw was a churning sea of emotions. I saw those gorgeous green eyes darkened with emotions but they were mixed and confusing. Or maybe he was just confused.

But then Drew's words came back to me. I heard them again as if he'd just said them aloud. *Because I wanted to.*

Without thinking it through any further, I took a deep breath and steadied my nerves. It was now or never. "Because I wanted to."

I blurted out his same answer because—well, because it was the truth. I'd loved that kiss. That kiss had been heaven on earth...until it had become hell on earth.

And now? Now I watched as some of the angst and the fear seeped out of his expression. The anger faded and the grin that he gave me was sexy beyond belief.

I swear, I could feel the effects of that smile in my toes. My breath caught in my throat as his eyes filled with a twinkling, mischievous laughter. "Well, all right then."

Something warm and infinitely sweet spread through my chest, making me feel full and content, and giddier than I ever knew I could be. "Well, all right then," I repeated, this time with a grin of my own.

He liked me. He might not have said it yet, but I knew it. I saw it—in his eyes and written all over his face.

This guy had feelings for me...and so did I.

Holy crap. Drew Remi likes me! That was pretty much the only thought my brain seemed capable of producing.

But then his expression fell, his brows pulling together. "I can't believe you thought I was pulling an Alex."

I bit my lip, guilt hitting me again like a punch in the gut. "Sorry," I muttered.

"Why would you even think that?" he asked. But before I could answer, he spoke again with a shake of his head. "No, I'm sorry."

"You are?"

"Why *wouldn't* you think that I'd pulled an Alex?" he said. "I never gave you any reason to think that I wanted anything more from you than friendship."

I arched my brows as the memory of that pizza conversation replayed in my head. "You did make it pretty clear you wanted to be friends and I—" I shifted from foot to foot. I had so much I wanted to say but no idea how. This was all new for me. All of it. For a moment it was too overwhelming.

"What?" he asked.

I snapped my head up to meet his gaze. Good grief, that gaze. It was lethal. *"What* what?" I asked stupidly.

He smirked, and for a second it actually put me at ease. He wasn't Drew Remi, superstar baseball player who was too-cool-for-school, he was just Drew. He was the guy I'd known forever and a guy I was friends with now.

Friends, but hopefully so much more.

"What what?" he repeated, openly mocking me for playing dumb.

That made me laugh, and whether it was weird or not, it put me even more at ease. Joking around with guys I could do, teasing wasn't hard. It was what I did with friends. And at the heart of it all, that's what we were. We were friends. And maybe more.

Hopefully more.

But a good relationship is rooted in friendship, right? So either way, we were friends.

That gave me the confidence to answer his not so eloquently phrased question. This was it, the moment of truth. I could either wuss out and officially play games...or I could be open and honest.

What I had to do was so obvious, but holy crap, it was so much easier said than done. Nevertheless, I did it. Because maybe I wasn't totally sure who I? was yet, but with perfect beach waves or a frizzy mass of curls pulled back in a ponytail, I wasn't a wuss and I didn't play games. That was a part of who I was, like it or not, and it wasn't going to change.

"You did say you wanted to be friends," I said. "I didn't think you were trying to be cruel by pulling an Alex, I just thought you were ignorant of certain key facts."

My voice trailed off with those lame words.

His lips were twitching with barely concealed amusement at my obvious discomfort. "Certain key facts," he repeated. I could see the strain it took for him to keep from laughing.

I rolled my eyes. "Yes, certain key facts. Namely, the fact that I liked you."

His amusement faded and the intensity of his stare made my mouth grew dry. "You liked me."

I let out a short exhale. "Are you going to keep repeating everything I say?"

He took a step toward me. We were standing so close I could smell peppermint on his breath, like he'd been chewing gum or just sucked on a mint. That combined with the scent of his soap and shampoo...it was like nature and Drew Remi had come together to create the headiest cocktail for one Veronica Smith.

"I'm only repeating the key facts," he teased, but there was that intensity there that belied his teasing tone. "You said you *liked* me. Past tense."

The question was there in the way his voice trailed off. It was there in his eyes as he waited for me to keep talking, as if my next words held the key his salvation. Being the sole object of this kind of focus was heady in its own way. I'd never before felt like the center of someone's universe, not until this particular moment.

I'd also never felt like the center of gravity in my own life had shifted to include someone else, but that's how it felt with Drew standing this close. We were in our own orbit.

I licked my lips, nervous even though I knew what he wanted to hear. "I like you," I said slowly. "Present tense."

The echoing silence lasted for a heartbeat but it felt like an eternity. And then he broke it with a loud groan as he reached for me and pulled me close so there was no air between us. "Oh thank God," he murmured before his mouth closed over mine.

This kiss was even better than the last. Maybe because this time there was no moment of shock, there was only sensation. Or maybe the kiss was so mind-blowing because I'd done it—I'd spoken the truth and said what I'd needed to say.

He hadn't, but I didn't even care. His kiss was answer enough. His lips were gentle and tender and passionate and rough. It[They? The kiss?] alternated between crazy intense and sweet, as though he was savoring every second, memorizing the feel of my lips, the taste of my tongue.

Were kisses always like this? Something told me no, probably not. When Drew finally came up for air, he basically told me so. Cupping my face between his palms, he looked at me like I was some precious treasure he'd just discovered, even though we both knew I'd been right in front of his face since birth, practically.

"I have never experienced a kiss like that."

See? He outright confirmed it. I knew that kiss was epic. I found myself grinning up at him like a moron. "It was pretty good, huh?"

"Good?" He arched his brows and feigned offense. "Good? Are you kidding me? That was amazing. Sensational. We should probably win awards for that kiss."

I nodded, even though he was still holding my face in his hands like he was afraid I'd run away again. "Oh, we would totally win in a kissing competition. If kissing was an Olympic event, we would be taking home the gold."

He laughed. "I'm so glad my girlfriend is just as competitive as I am."

My mind went blank. "Girlfriend?" It came out as a squeak.

He winced, probably because of the squeak. "Too soon to use the g-word?"

I blinked a few times as if that might help my brain to process what had just happened. I'm pretty sure my brain was still stuck on the fact that Drew Remi had kissed me. It had so not caught up to the rest. I could barely breathe when I thought of the way I'd outright told him I like him. Or the way he'd kissed me after.

Or the way he was looking at me right now.

Looking, but not talking. I gently pushed his hands away and took two steps back. It wasn't easy when my body was begging to get even closer. My body definitely wanted me to leap into his arms, not back away.

He frowned. "What are you doing?"

"I'm trying to think," I said. "And I'm having a hard enough time doing that without you being all..." I gestured to his hot, sexy self. "You."

He smirked. Man, that smirk was hot.

"I think you might need to turn around," I said. "I need a moment."

His smirk grew to an all out grin that slayed me to my core. I was a goner. Stick a fork in me because I was done. This guy owned my soul with that smile.

Instead of turning around he took a step in my direction and then another, moving slowly and with exaggerated long steps just like I'd done when I'd backed away. "What are you doing?" I asked. "You're supposed to be giving me space. You're supposed to turn around."

He nodded but he did neither of those things. He moved so close I may have been able to name the flavor and brand of his gum. Peppermint Orbit, in case you were wondering.

"I want to see the look in your eyes when I tell you how I feel about you," he said softly, simply, like it was the easiest thing in the world.

I kind of wished I had a redo for my own little speech. He made being forthright look so graceful and easy, not like my awkward, clumsy attempt. It was at this point that I realized just how accurate he was about our competitive compatibility.

I clasped my hands in front of me to keep from reaching out to him or touching him in some way. Now that I'd been so close to him and had permission to touch him again, withholding from that sort of intimacy felt stupidly hard.

I swallowed down a wave of nerves. "And how do you feel about me?"

He waited until my eyes locked with his before reaching out and brushing some hair away from my face. "I like you, Veronica Smith." His mouth hitched up in a cute lopsided grin. "I more than like you, if I'm being honest. But I don't want to scare you away by moving too fast."

I nodded, trying to stay calm even as my heart tried to make a run for it. Not because I was scared. I wasn't. I was excited, and overwhelmed, and...yeah, okay, maybe a little scared. "I've never..." I gestured toward him and then to me. "I've never..."

He arched a brow as he wrapped his arms around me, pulling me back into his arms. Back where I belonged.

There I went again, psyching myself out. This time I felt a thrill of excitement, a surge of belonging I hadn't known I'd been missing. I'd found someone who saw me. The real me. The me I wasn't even sure I saw so clearly myself. But he did. When I looked into his eyes, I felt more sure of myself. Not because the hottie baseball star liked me, but because my mind stopped the overanalyzing and the doubting when I looked into his eyes.

I was just...me. Ronnie and Veronica. Good athlete and girly blushing idiot, at least when he was around. I was a work in progress, but so was he. I'd changed over the years and so had he. And I liked the person he'd become, and apparently he felt the same about me.

He was still waiting for me to finish what I'd started to say. "I've never done anything like this before."

He leaned down and pressed a light kiss to my lips. "You've never made out in a parking lot in front of the entire student body before?"

I jerked my head back in surprise and turned to face the diner. Sure enough we were putting on a show for everyone inside. Through the glass windows I could see a million faces turned in our direction staring. My gasp turned into a laugh even as my cheeks burst into flames.

I buried my head in Drew's chest to hide from the peering eyes and felt his laughter beneath my cheek. "This is so embarrassing," I mumbled.

He laughed harder. "Why? Are you embarrassed to be seen with me?"

I smacked his chest and pulled back far enough to scowl at him. "You know what I mean."

His grin was so self-satisfied I had to roll my eyes. "You're enjoying this, aren't you?"

"Of course." He leaned down so his lips were close to my ear. "The hot new girl is my girlfriend, and now everyone knows it."

I shivered at the words as much as his tone. I was his girlfriend. That was a new way of seeing myself that was definitely going to take some getting used to. It was new term for me, but I liked it already.

"What did you really mean before?" he asked. "You've never done what before? Had a boyfriend?"

I could feel that stupid heat in my cheeks and was suddenly grateful for the darkness. Our audience might have gotten quite a show but at least they wouldn't see me blush. I hereby solemnly vow that Drew Remi would be the only person to ever see me blush.

I nodded. "I've never had a boyfriend before." I swallowed down my embarrassment as I admitted the next part. "I've also never..."

He arched a brow and tightened his arms around me. "You've also never...what?"

I wrinkled my nose and forced out the rest. "I've also never been kissed before?" My voice went weirdly up at the end like it was a question. Ugh, this was humiliating.

When I finally summoned the courage to look at Drew, my heart melted in my chest. He looked shocked, and rightfully so. I was probably the last girl in our class to have her first kiss, at Atwater or Briarwood.

But beyond the shock was something so unbearably

tender, it made a gooey, sticky-sweet warmth spread throughout my whole body. Finally I shifted in his arms at his silence. "Say something."

He leaned down and rested his forehead against mine. "I'm honored to be your first kiss, Ronnie."

The use of my old nickname made me smile. I liked the fact that he remembered who I was—that he wasn't just kissing the new and improved Veronica, but the tomboy he'd known forever as well.

The hot new girl. His earlier words came back to me and made me grin. Yeah, I guess he'd kissed her too.

EPILOGUE

Drew

HERE'S the thing about my girlfriend—she's competitive in the extreme. I led our baseball team to win the playoffs, so what did she do? She took her soccer team to state.

Half the school turned out to watch them win, but when she came out of the locker room afterward, she sought me out in the crowd, just like she's the person I look for first anytime I walk into a room. It's always been like that between us, ever since we made our relationship official back in the fall of our junior year. Now we're seniors and graduation will be coming up before we know it.

I wave her down and she fights her way through a crowd of classmates who are vying for her attention outside the locker rooms. She's nice about it, but she's steadily making her way over to me, where I'm waiting with Trent and Margo. The four of us made plans to go out afterward to celebrate her win.

Or commiserate her loss, she'd been quick to add before

tonight's game. Apparently my superstitious nature has rubbed off on her.

But her team won so we'll be celebrating along with the rest of the school. Funny that after all her efforts to be the kind of popular girl she thought people would like, Veronica is beloved at Briarwood thanks to her mad skills on the field.

When she reaches my side, she's still sweaty from kicking ass out on the field. Her hair is pulled back out of her face and she's beaming over her victory. Honestly, she has never been more beautiful. I draw her in for a kiss that leaves us both out of breath and aching for more.

But she's got friends to greet and a team to celebrate with, and we've got all the time in the world to be together. I guess it's obvious that I've had a change of heart about high school relationships. Maybe they're not all doomed to failure. Being with Veronica has made me optimistic like that.

She's also turned me into quite the romantic. I love surprising her and coming up with new ways to make her blush. It drives her crazy, which makes it all the more rewarding.

I've got a big surprise planned for her later tonight, because I've got news of my own to celebrate. After what feels like the longest wait of my life, I got my acceptance letter to Boston University today. Veronica had gotten early acceptance to Boston College, where she received a soccer scholarship. We'd been hoping to stay near each other when we went off to college, and now we would.

Don't get me wrong. If there was any relationship that could handle long distance, it was ours. But I didn't want to be away from Veronica. Not now, and hopefully not ever. It's a crazy feeling when you find your best friend and the love of your life in one person, and that's what I have in Veronica.

We get a lot of flak from people who say that young love doesn't last. *You'll change*, they tell us. *You'll grow apart.*

Here's the thing that Veronica helped me realize. We're always changing. We're always growing. It didn't mean that we had to be moving in different directions, not as long as we support one another and give each other room to grow.

But the thing people don't always understand is that Veronica helps me to be the kind of man I want to be. She sees the best in me, just like I see that in her. When we're together we're the very best versions of ourselves.

She wraps one arm around my waist as Trent and Margo come over to congratulate her on the win. I wait patiently for her to accept the praise she's so rightfully due, and when we're alone once again, I seize my chance and steal another kiss.

"What was that for?" she asks with a grin.

"I'm so proud of you," I say.

Her smile grows as she leans in for another quick kiss. "I wish we could celebrate by ourselves for a little while."

I give her a squeeze. "Later," I promise. "But right now you deserve to revel in your win. Besides, there's a school full of people who want to tell you how amazing you are."

She rolls her eyes, but she's still smiling. With a fake sigh, she says, "It's so hard to be loved. How do you do it all the time?"

I laugh at her teasing, because I know as well as she does that she's just as beloved as I am, if not more so. But the funniest part is, she doesn't care about any of that anymore and neither do I. It feels so long ago that any of that was important, even though it was only last year. Since then she's realized that she was never invisible, not in any way that mattered, just like I realized that being popular wasn't the same as having good friends.

With an arm around her shoulders, I lead her toward the crowd who's waiting to talk to her. She might not care about being popular anymore, but I'm glad for her sake that she's finally being recognized for her talents and for her beautiful personality.

She squeezes my waist as one of her teammates beckons for her to join them. Looking up at me with those warm brown eyes, she asks, "We'll celebrate together later?"

I drop a kiss on top of her head. "Of course." Then with a grin I add, "You and I have all the time in the world."

THANK YOU FOR READING! Continue the Briarwood High series with the next book, *A Whole New League*. Turn the page for a free sample!

THE STAR QUARTERBACK **dating a theater geek like me? As if anyone would believe that...**

IF BRIAN KIRKLAND is the reigning king of the jocks, I guess that makes me the queen of the drama department. Hard to believe we were ever best friends.

These days we go to great lengths to ignore one another. But when Brian's diva girlfriend convinces him to try out for my play, there's no way to avoid him.

I try to keep it professional, but years of anger and resentment are hard to dismiss. It doesn't help that he's just as cocky as I remember. He lives to antagonize me, which is why I'm just as stunned as everyone else when he does something nice. Something...unexpected.

His very public kiss is an act of kindness to save me from humiliation, but it leads the entire school to think that we're dating. Which is just crazy...right?

A WHOLE NEW LEAGUE
BRIARWOOD HIGH #2

Alice

THE STADIUM SEAT beneath me shook from all the pounding and the clapping in Briarwood High's large gymnasium. I held onto my seat and rolled my eyes. "Neanderthals," I muttered, too quietly for anyone to hear. Not even my friend Julian who sat beside me and clearly shared my disgust.

Of course he did, that was why we were friends.

"Look at them," he said, nodding toward the double doors where the football players streamed in, throwing their arms up as they encouraged the crowd.

Ugh, I hated football players. Even worse, I hated these tedious school assemblies that we were forced to participate in to show our school spirit.

School spirit was for suckers. Assemblies like this were a sort of brainwashing technique schools used to try and enforce a sense of bonding and camaraderie amongst us students.

I'd been going to Briarwood since kindergarten, I think it was safe to say that if I didn't feel a bond with my fellow classmates by our senior year, it probably wasn't going to happen.

My eyes narrowed as one by one these high school "heroes" made their grand entrance, grinning at the catcalls and cheers as though they'd honestly done something of value that warranted this sort of attention.

What did they do? They threw a ball around. *Whoop de doo.* The cheers picked up a notch and I winced as my headache grew in direct proportion to the crowd's noisy chants. What was the uptick in cheering for? I didn't even have to look to know. Everyone's favorite player had just arrived.

Brian Kirkland. King jock, cocky jerk...and my former best friend.

We used to be neighbors. Actually, we were still neighbors but it was easy to forget since we'd gotten good at ignoring one another's existence. We also used to be inseparable—right up until junior high. One day he was my kind, funny friend Brian and the next he'd shot up into a gigantic brick wall and his ego grew even bigger.

He'd become a football star seemingly overnight. With his dark hair and eyes, classic All-American good looks, and easy confidence, he was instantly beloved. But worse, much worse, he'd become friends with the kids who'd ignored us in elementary school. Suddenly he was too cool to hang out with me, and all signs of intellect and humor vanished beneath that dopey perma-grin that had enchanted everyone in this school.

Everyone but me.

All guys wanted to be him, all girls wanted to date him. He was your classic teenage horror show.

There were some supremely lonely years after Brian ditched me for the cool crowd, but luckily Julian transferred to our school last year and we hit it off instantly. He's one of very few people I actually liked in this school. No, that wasn't fair—I liked a lot of kids, just none of the ones we were supposed to be cheering for today.

"What are we supposed to be honoring them for?" I asked, honestly perplexed. "It's not like they've found the cure for cancer, they've just won some games."

Julian was the only person I could say stuff like this to. Thankfully he came to our school. I finally had someone in my life who understood me.

And that right there was the reason I couldn't bring myself to make a move.

I had a thing for my friend. Cliché and predictable, I know, but there it was. He was cute in a dorky emo kind of way. Lanky and tall, with dark-framed glasses and a jaded sarcasm that perfectly matched my own. Sitting next to one another, we must have made quite the geeky pair. Him with his glasses and ironic T-shirts and me with my oversized cardigans and blonde hair twisted up in knots on top of my head. No matter how I tried to keep it back, wispy strands always managed to float down around my face. *Fine hair*, my mom's hairdresser called it. I called it thin and uncooperative. It was a white-blonde and always had been. Like everything else about me, my hair seemed to get stunted in my youth. It looked exactly the same as it did in the fifth grade. Sadly, everything else about me stayed the same too. I was still holding out hope that boobs and butt were coming my way, but I wasn't expecting much.

However, as my little sister liked to point out, it wouldn't matter even if I did get curves since my clothes were on the loose side anyways. Oversized sweaters and slouchy jeans were pretty much my uniform.

I was fine with my look—except for the boobs and butt thing. Those would be nice, if for no other reason than I might actually start to look my age. I could drive a car yet I'd recently been given a hard time by a ticket taker for attempting to see a PG-13 movie on my own.

So embarrassing.

But back to my point—I was pretty certain Julian and I stuck out as the dweebs we were, but honestly, I wouldn't have had it any other way. I was still thankful I wasn't sitting alone at this assembly like I had freshman and sophomore year, before Julian had arrived.

He hated this crowd as much as I did. That alone would have made us friends. But the fact that he was also into art and music had sealed the deal. It wasn't easy to find creative types in our school, which valued brute strength and mindless athleticism over anything with substance and soul.

You're probably thinking—*jaded much*? Yeah, I know. But you would be too if you went to a school where the dumbest and most shallow of the bunch were considered gods, and the rest of us were invisible or mocked. Sometimes both depending on the day.

Julian leaned over to be heard over the crowd. "Next week I'm throwing you a school assembly."

His tone was so serious, I was already grinning. "Oh yeah?"

He nodded somberly. "A parade, really."

"That sounds nice," I said, playing along. "What did I do to deserve such an honor?"

He looked me straight in the eyes and I felt a sudden onset of nerves. "You got an *A* in algebra."

I laughed. "I totally did! Why aren't we celebrating *me* right now?"

His somber expression gave way to a super cute smile. "I know, right?" Then, just as I thought we might be having a moment here, what with the teasing and the unbroken eye contact, he leaned over and nudged my shoulder in a decidedly friendly fashion. "Seriously, though. You should get mad props for winning that playwriting contest."

And just like that my cheeks were on fire.

I looked down at the football players gathered below and tried to ignore the couple who'd started making out next to me. That's what you get when you opted for the nosebleed seats in the school's gymnasium. Some of us came up here to get away from the mindless mob and others...I snuck a quick peek at them going at it, devouring one another's tongues like cannibals.

Well, some came up here to get some action, apparently.

Not us, though. Julian's attention was back on the assembly below too. If he was tempted to sneak in a kiss while the rest of the school participated in brainwashing exercises, he showed no hint of it.

It was official. I would never be kissed.

I sighed before rolling my eyes at my own idiocy. I would be kissed—and often—once I got out of this fishbowl called Briarwood High and our small town.

"Are you coming to Java Hut tonight?" Julian asked.

Every Wednesday night a local coffee shop held open mic night and Julian liked to try out his new songs. I gave him a regretful wince. "I'd love to but auditions start tonight for the female lead."

Ever since freshman year I'd been the stage manager for every show our school's theater department put on. It was a small department, not nearly as well supported as other after-school activities like, say, football. But we did our best. As an aspiring playwright and potential screenwriter, I loved the backstage element, learning the craft by watching it in action.

Mr. Brenner, the director and head of the theater department, was fun to work with, too. He was like a kid himself sometimes. If Julian hadn't come along, Mr. Brenner probably would have been my only friend. Pathetic, right?

"Who are they casting tonight?" Julian asked.

"Gwendolyn," I said. I knew without having to ask that Julian had read *The Importance of Being Earnest*. He'd probably read it even before finding out that I'd be stage managing the production, but knowing that I'd be working on it I knew without a doubt that he'd read it. Not only was he wonderfully literate, my crush was also an excellent friend. He would be perfection personified if he would just kiss me already.

"You should audition," Julian said. I jerked back in surprise at that. "Me? Why?"

"You'd make a great Gwendolyn," he said with a shrug, seemingly not noticing my open-mouthed stare that clearly called him crazy.

"I don't act," I said.

He glanced over. "You could."

"No, I couldn't," I said. Frankly I wasn't even sure why we were talking about this. My role was backstage, out of sight. Always had been and always would be. I'd never liked the spotlight, I just liked the words and the way actors and directors could bring them to life.

I knew it sounded cheesy, but it always felt like magic,

watching words turn into tangible action and emotions. It was a form of wizardry, as far as I was concerned.

I would never say that out loud, of course. I realized how corny it sounded.

"Have you ever thought about it?" he asked.

"About *acting*?" I imbued the word with all the disbelief I was feeling. But seriously, how had he known me for this long and not know how much I hated to be the center of attention?

He nodded.

"No. Definitely not." I shook my head with a little too much vehemence and a thick strand of hair slid out from a hair clip and fell into my face. "Besides, the part is as good as cast," I said, wanting to get the focus off me and his terrifically terrible idea that I audition.

He arched his brows in question.

"Hayley Hayes," I said.

His brows lifted even higher in understanding. "Ah."

"Exactly."

Hayley was another senior and the school's leading diva. She'd been cast as the lead female character in every play or musical for the past two years.

Her streak would not die today.

Julian wrinkled his nose, forming a crinkle at the bridge where his glasses rested. "I don't think she's all that great."

Me neither. "She's the best we've got."

"Then it's slim pickings around here," he said, his tone decisive. Julian had judged the quality of potential actors at Briarwood and found them lacking.

I made a noncommittal noise. I didn't feel like arguing the point, but I wasn't so certain that was true. Hayley wasn't the best, but she wasn't the worst either. She had charisma and enthusiasm on stage, but she didn't take it as seriously as I would have liked.

In short, she lacked in the work ethic department.

Her talent for actual acting was so-so, but since she clearly wasn't harboring hopes of going pro. I supposed she did just fine for what she was aiming for, which was good for a high school production.

But what Julian didn't seem to get was that Hayley's mediocre talent wasn't the only reason she got the leading role. There was one other major factor that came into play, probably more than her skills on the stage.

She was popular. Pretty in a Blair Waldorf sort of way, she had the school wrapped around her perky little finger. How did that factor into her leading lady status? Well, the looks part was obvious...I mean, we could talk until we're blue in the face about how talent mattered more than looks, but this was the real world and like it or not, it was hard to ignore a beautiful girl on stage, especially when her competition paled in comparison.

But then there was the fact that our department was underfunded and constantly struggling. Like a mini version of Broadway, our little stage also had to resort to hiring A-listers to headline in order to ensure the seats were packed.

Oh, no one ever outright admitted this. Mr. Brenner would rather eat his clipboard than admit that he'd cast a lead role based on anything other than talent. But I knew that was a factor.

And last but not least, Hayley's popularity and that charming confidence did an amazing job of eliminating her competition before auditions even began. I'd already heard two of our regular actresses moaning about how they'd love to play Gwendolyn, but why should they bother when Hayley Hayes was auditioning.

Instead both girls were vying for the role of Cecily, though I was pretty sure neither of them was quite right. But that would be up to Mr. Brenner, I was just there to take notes and hand out scripts.

I was thinking about how many copies I'd have to make for tonight's auditions when Julian interrupted my thoughts.

"She would make a perfect Gwendolyn, wouldn't she?" he mused.

I followed his gaze and saw that Hayley was below us, directly in our line of vision but in the second row, where she would have a good view of her boyfriend. The king jock himself, Brian Kirkland.

Ugh. Excuse me while I gagged. If ever there was a more obnoxiously atrocious couple than Brian and Hayley, I couldn't imagine it. They were like stereotypes of themselves—the charming, smarmy, egotistical jock and his smiley, dramatic, gorgeous diva girlfriend.

Diva. That's exactly what she was. She had this way of walking with her chin tilted up in the air as if she were trying to see over the rest of us peons. She was the perfect fit for Brian with his giant ego.

Their combined confidence could conquer the world... or, at the very least, win homecoming king and queen.

I watched her beaming with pride below, as she clapped and cheered. There was something about it that felt so feigned. I always got this sense around her, like she was constantly performing even when she wasn't on stage. I could practically see her inner monologue right now. *Are they watching? They'd better be watching. I'm the epitome of a supportive girlfriend. See? Just look at how encouraging I am.*

And I'm sure Brian just ate it up. He wouldn't care if

her accolades were fake or not, as long as it was keeping that ego well fed with a steady diet of flattery and charm.

God, they were truly nauseating.

Watching Hayley I realized that Julian was spot on in his assessment. The character of Gwendolyn was all about style over substance.

Hayley was the perfect fit.

Our bigger problem was who to cast as Ernest. The obvious choice had graduated and our little theater world was still mourning the loss. It was hard enough to get guys interested in plays, but guys who were actually good?

Almost impossible.

I was still watching Hayley play the role of Hayley Hayes, supportive girlfriend, when Brian broke away from his teammates to go to her, bending down to give her a quick kiss that made the entire auditorium erupt with gleeful laughter and loud teasing.

Julian gave me a droll look that was far more expressive than any eye roll. I laughed in response, but my insides were twisting in that familiar way. This was why I went out of my way to avoid Brian Kirkland. Everything he did made me angry beyond reason. Like that kiss. Was that really necessary? Was he not getting enough attention with this freakin' assembly that he had to hog even more of the spotlight?

This was yet another reason I hated these stupid required assemblies. Every other day of the year I went out of my way to avoid my former best friend, not too difficult since we ran in different circles, but events like this made it impossible.

"Looks like they've cinched it," Julian said in that dry tone I loved so much.

I nodded. I knew exactly what he was talking about.

We'd been joking ever since homecoming court was announced that the contenders were secretly battling it out *Hunger Games*-style to win the coveted crown. "Oh yeah. They've just slaughtered the competition. It's a bloody battlefield out there. Carnage everywhere." I took on a wrestling announcer's voice as though we were really at a sporting event and not some weird build-up to one. "Ladies and gentlemen, your new homecoming king and queen."

Julian cupped his hands around his mouth and made fake crowd sounds that were nearly drowned out by the real crowd sounds.

We were both laughing at our own stupid joke, but I caught Brian's gloating grin as he made his way back to his team, acknowledging the good-natured shouts and laughter as though he'd truly just done something spectacular

That guy seriously lived for praise and adoration. He accepted it as if it was his due. My hands clenched in my lap as the familiar irritation swept over me at the sight of that smirk. He was a male diva—the king jock version of Hayley's shining starlet. Brian Kirkland hogged the spotlight more than anyone I knew.

Thank God he'd never decided to take up acting.

TO KEEP READING, check out *A Whole New League*.

ABOUT THE AUTHOR

MAGGIE DALLEN IS a big city girl living in Montana. She writes romantic comedies in a range of genres including young adult, historical, contemporary, and fantasy. An unapologetic addict of all things romance, she loves to connect with fellow avid readers. Subscribe to her newsletter at http://eepurl.com/bFEVsL

Made in the USA
Columbia, SC
16 June 2025